ELYSIAN ECHOES

THE GUARDIAN'S JOURNEY

MISHKA JAIN

For those who dare to dream,

For the brave hearts who stand against the darkness,

And for my family and friends,

whose unwavering support and love illuminate my path.

This journey is for you.

Contents

Contents

Foreword

In a world where shadows loom and hope flickers like a candle in the dark, the story of Eldara unfolds—a tale that explores the eternal struggle between light and darkness, courage and fear, friendship and betrayal. This narrative invites readers into a realm brimming with magic, mystery, and the indomitable spirit of those who refuse to yield to despair.

As you embark on this journey with Lira and her friends, you will witness their evolution from ordinary individuals into extraordinary heroes. Each character grapples with their own fears and insecurities, ultimately discovering that true strength lies not in isolation but in the bonds forged through shared experiences. It is a poignant reminder that, even in our darkest moments, we can find solace and resilience through connection and trust.

The world of Eldara is rich with vibrant landscapes, mystical creatures, and ancient legends. It reflects the beauty and complexity of our own world while allowing us to explore the deeper truths of humanity through the lens of fantasy. Through trials and triumphs, the characters will face moral dilemmas that challenge their beliefs and force them to confront the very essence of what it means to be brave.

This story serves as both an escape and a mirror, reminding us that the battles we fight, whether internal or external, shape who we are. As you turn the pages, I encourage you to reflect on your own journey and the light that guides you through your challenges.

Thank you for joining me in this adventure. May the tale of Lira and her companions inspire you to embrace your own light, even when darkness threatens to engulf it.

Preface

Welcome to the world of Eldara, a realm where light and darkness are in a constant struggle for balance. This story began as a spark of inspiration, born from a love of adventure and a fascination with the extraordinary. It is a tale of courage, friendship, and the unyielding spirit of those who dare to stand against the shadows.

As you journey through these pages, you will meet Lira and her companions—each with their own unique strengths and challenges. Together, they will confront the encroaching darkness known as the Shade, a force that seeks to extinguish the light of hope that has nurtured their land for generations. But this is not just a battle against an external enemy; it is also a journey of self-discovery and growth as they learn to harness their powers, confront their fears, and trust in one another.

In writing this story, I sought to explore the themes of resilience and the power of connection. The characters' struggles reflect our own journeys, reminding us that even in the face of adversity, we can find strength in unity and hope in the darkest of times.

I invite you to immerse yourself in the enchanting landscapes of Eldara, from its mystical forests to the shimmering lakes. Let the magic of this world captivate you, and may you find inspiration in the challenges faced by Lira and her friends.

Thank you for joining me on this adventure. I hope that you will find as much joy in reading this story as I did in writing it.

Acknowledgements

Acknowledgments

First and foremost, I would like to extend my deepest gratitude to my family and friends for their unwavering support and encouragement throughout the journey of writing this book. Your belief in my abilities kept me motivated during the toughest days.

To the mentors and authors who inspired me along the way, thank you for your stories and your guidance. Your words fueled my imagination and encouraged me to pursue my passion for storytelling.

I would also like to acknowledge the countless individuals who share their knowledge and creativity in the world of literature and art. You have made the realm of fantasy richer and more vibrant.

Lastly, to the readers—thank you for embarking on this journey with me. I hope that the world of Eldara, with its trials and triumphs, resonates with you as much as it does with me. Your support means everything, and I am excited to share this adventure with you.

Prologue

Prologue

In a realm where shadows lurked just beyond the reach of light, the world was on the brink of chaos. The land of Eldara had once thrived under the protective gaze of the ancient Heartstone, a powerful gem said to hold the essence of life itself. Its radiant glow warded off darkness, nurturing the forests, rivers, and the hearts of its people. But as time passed, the Heartstone's light began to fade, and with it, the encroaching darkness grew bolder.

Whispers of an ancient evil known as the Shade spread like wildfire. Legends told of a malevolent force that thrived on fear and despair, seeking to extinguish the light that gave Eldara its life. It crept into the hearts of men, turning allies against one another and sowing discord among friends. Villages fell silent, their inhabitants consumed by an overwhelming dread, as shadows deepened and hope diminished.

Yet, amidst the growing despair, a flicker of hope emerged. A group of unlikely heroes, bound by fate, rose to confront the darkness. Lira, a young woman with a mysterious connection to the Heartstone, felt the weight of destiny on her shoulders. With her friends—Orion, a fierce protector; Kiran, a skilled strategist; and Anya, a healer—Lira was determined to reignite the light of the Heartstone and restore balance to Eldara.

As they journeyed into the heart of the darkness, they would face trials that tested their strength, their bonds, and their resolve. Each challenge would force them to confront their fears, unravel secrets long buried, and discover the true meaning of courage and friendship. Little did they know that the greatest battles would not only be against the Shade but within themselves.

The fate of Eldara rested in their hands, and as the first tendrils of darkness began to creep into their lives, Lira and her friends prepared to embark on a quest that would change their world forever. With hearts ablaze with hope and determination, they stepped into the unknown, ready to reclaim the light.

1

The Dreamweaver's Guild

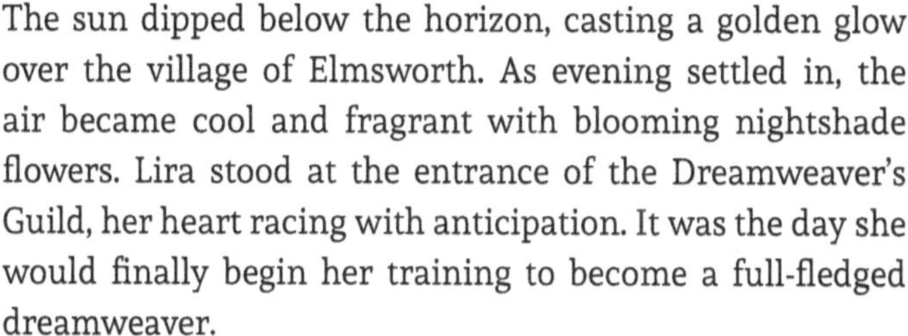

The sun dipped below the horizon, casting a golden glow over the village of Elmsworth. As evening settled in, the air became cool and fragrant with blooming nightshade flowers. Lira stood at the entrance of the Dreamweaver's Guild, her heart racing with anticipation. It was the day she would finally begin her training to become a full-fledged dreamweaver.

Inside the guild, the scent of incense wafted through the air, mingling with the soft glow of luminescent orbs suspended from the ceiling. Dreamweavers bustled about, their robes swirling like clouds, each one lost in the ethereal world of dreams. Lira's mentor, Master Aelion, a tall man with silver hair and piercing blue eyes, stood at the center of the grand hall, surrounded by vibrant tapestries depicting fantastical dreams.

"Lira!" Master Aelion called, his voice booming yet warm. "Welcome to your first day as an apprentice. Today, we will begin your journey into the realm of dreams."

Lira stepped forward, her heart fluttering. "Thank you, Master Aelion. I'm ready to learn."

The master smiled, his eyes twinkling with wisdom. "To be a dreamweaver, you must understand the delicate balance between dreams and reality. Our craft is not merely about weaving beautiful dreams; it's about helping others confront their fears, desires, and the shadows lurking within their minds."

As he spoke, Lira's thoughts wandered to her own nightmares, the ones that haunted her since childhood—dark figures that whispered secrets and laughter, urging her to forget. She shuddered, pushing the memories aside. This was her chance to create something beautiful, to transform darkness into light.

Master Aelion motioned for Lira to follow him to the Dream Chamber, a vast room filled with swirling mist and glowing crystals. "Today, we'll start with the Dream Essence Collection. Each essence holds the power to influence dreams. Some inspire courage, while others can provoke fear."

Lira watched in awe as the master demonstrated, his hands weaving through the air. Wisps of light swirled around him, forming delicate strands that shimmered like starlight. With a swift motion, he captured a glowing essence in a crystal vial. "Feel the essence, understand its nature, and learn to harness its power."

Taking a deep breath, Lira stepped forward and closed her eyes. She reached out with her senses, feeling the pull of the essences around her. Suddenly, a flicker of darkness brushed against her thoughts, sending a shiver down her spine. Startled, she opened her eyes, but it was gone.

"Are you all right?" Master Aelion's voice broke through her concentration.

"Yes, just a moment," she replied, shaking off the lingering chill. "I felt something... strange."

"Trust your instincts," he encouraged. "The realm of dreams is unpredictable. Shadows can reveal truths, but they can also mislead."

Determined to focus, Lira continued her practice, slowly learning to weave the essences into delicate patterns. Hours passed, and as the sun fully set, the Dream Chamber filled with an enchanting glow.

Suddenly, a loud crash echoed from the entrance. Lira turned, startled. A figure stumbled through the doorway, his silhouette framed by the fading light. He was tall, with tousled dark hair and a cloak that appeared to shimmer like starlit skies. His eyes, bright and piercing, locked onto hers.

"Lira," he said, breathless, as if he had been searching for her. "You need to come with me. The dreams are changing, and something terrible is coming."

Lira's heart raced. She had never seen this man before, yet there was something familiar about him, a spark that ignited an inexplicable connection. "Who are you?" she demanded, uncertainty flooding her voice.

"I'm Orion," he replied, stepping closer. "And I need your help."

As Lira stood on the threshold between the safety of the guild and the unknown world beyond, a strange mix of fear and excitement coursed through her veins. She had trained her entire life for this moment, but never could she have imagined the journey that awaited her—or the bond she would forge with the enigmatic stranger before her.

"Lead the way," she finally said, her heart pounding with a mix of courage and curiosity.

With one last glance at the warm glow of the guild, Lira stepped into the shadows, ready to unravel the mysteries of the realm of dreams and the echoes of her own heart.

2

The Shattered Realm

Lira stepped out of the Dreamweaver's Guild and into the cool evening air, her heart racing as she followed Orion into the depths of the darkening woods. The familiar path behind her faded, replaced by the dense shadows of towering trees. Whispers of wind rustled through the leaves, carrying an eerie melody that sent shivers down her spine.

"What do you mean, 'something terrible is coming'?" Lira asked, glancing at Orion, who walked with an air of urgency. His cloak fluttered behind him like a shadow, and she found herself captivated by the way he moved, each step purposeful and sure.

Orion cast a glance over his shoulder, his expression serious. "The dreams are being corrupted. Nightmares are spilling into the waking world, affecting everyone in Elmsworth. I came to warn you because I believe you hold the key to stopping it."

"Me? Why me?" Lira questioned, disbelief creeping into her voice. She had always felt a connection to dreams, but she never thought of herself as anything special—just another apprentice in the guild.

"Your talent as a dreamweaver is stronger than you realize. The essence you create can heal the rifts in the dream realm. But first, we need to gather the lost fragments of the goddess's heart," he explained, urgency lacing his words.

Lira furrowed her brow. "The goddess's heart? What are you talking about?"

Orion paused, turning to face her fully. "Long ago, the goddess of dreams was betrayed by her lover, and in her anguish, she shattered her heart into three fragments to protect the dream realm from darkness. Those fragments are hidden, but they hold immense power. If we don't find them, the nightmares will consume everything."

The weight of his words hung in the air like a storm cloud. Lira's mind raced as she processed the implications. "How do we find these fragments? Where do we start?"

"We'll begin in the Forgotten Village. It's rumored that the first fragment lies within a dream lost to time, buried in the memories of the villagers," Orion said, his eyes gleaming with determination. "But we must be careful. The darkness has a way of twisting the minds of those who dwell too long in it."

They moved deeper into the forest, the moonlight filtering through the leaves, casting silver beams upon the ground. As they walked, Lira felt the weight of uncertainty pressing against her chest. She had trained for years in the guild, yet this felt different—dangerous, exhilarating, and inexplicably tied to the stranger at her side.

"Tell me about yourself, Orion," Lira said, breaking the silence. "How do you know all of this?"

Orion hesitated for a moment, as if weighing his words. "I was once a guardian of dreams. I watched over the dream realm, ensuring that nightmares didn't spill into the waking world. But when the goddess was betrayed, I lost my powers, along with my connection to the dreams. I have been searching for a way to restore balance ever since."

His admission struck a chord in Lira's heart. She could sense the burden he carried, the weight of responsibility. "But why did you come to me? Why not someone else?"

"Because I felt your presence," he replied, his gaze piercing into hers. "When I sensed the disturbance in the dream realm, it led me to you. You are different, Lira. There's a strength within you that resonates with the essence of dreams. You're destined for more than you realize."

As they neared the edge of the forest, the trees thinned, revealing the outlines of crumbling cottages in the distance. The Forgotten Village lay before them, shrouded in a mist that clung to the ground like a whispered memory.

Lira's heart raced as they approached the village square, where the remnants of once-vibrant life now lay dormant. Broken carts and faded signs stood as relics of a past long forgotten. The air felt heavy with unspoken stories, and Lira could sense the lingering echoes of dreams gone awry.

"Stay close," Orion murmured, scanning the area with a wary expression. "We'll need to find someone who remembers the dreams of this place. They hold the key to locating the first heart fragment."

As they stepped further into the village, Lira felt an unsettling chill wrap around her, as if the shadows themselves were watching. Her instincts kicked in, and she tightened her grip on her dreamweaver's talisman—a small crystal pendant that had been her only link to the guild.

Suddenly, a figure emerged from the mist, an old woman hunched over with age. Her eyes, sharp and piercing, regarded Lira and Orion with a mix of curiosity and caution.

"Who are you, and what brings you to this forsaken place?" the woman rasped, her voice a harsh whisper.

"We seek the dreams of this village," Lira replied, her voice steady despite the unease settling in her stomach. "We're searching for the first fragment of the goddess's heart."

The old woman's eyes narrowed, as if searching Lira's soul. "Many have sought the dreams here, but they are lost. The darkness has claimed them. You'll need more than courage to uncover the truth."

Orion stepped forward, determination etched on his face. "We're not afraid of the darkness. We will find the lost dreams and restore what was broken."

The woman's lips curled into a faint smile, revealing a glimmer of hope amidst her weariness. "Then you must enter the Dreamweaver's Sanctuary. It is where the dreams lie hidden, but beware—the shadows guard them fiercely."

Lira exchanged a glance with Orion, their resolve solidifying. They had come too far to turn back now. Together, they would face the shadows and uncover the truth behind the shattered realm.

As they ventured toward the sanctuary, Lira felt a strange sense of destiny unfurling before her—a path woven from dreams, courage, and the spark of something deeper, something that connected her to the enigmatic stranger beside her.

3

An Unexpected Encounter

The Dreamweaver's Sanctuary loomed before Lira and Orion, a crumbling structure entwined with vines and shadow. Its entrance, framed by ancient stone, beckoned them with an eerie allure. As they approached, the air thickened with the scent of forgotten dreams—sweet and haunting, like the memories of a distant lullaby.

"Are you ready?" Orion asked, his voice steady but his eyes reflecting a hint of apprehension.

Lira nodded, steeling herself for what lay ahead. "We have to find the lost dreams. It's our only chance to locate the heart fragment."

They stepped into the sanctuary, crossing a threshold where light and shadow danced together. The interior was dimly lit, illuminated by flickering candles that cast elongated shadows across the walls. Murals depicting dreamscapes—mountains of cotton candy, rivers of starlight, and fields of wildflowers—decorated the space, each image a portal to another world.

"Look," Lira murmured, pointing to a mural depicting a dreamer standing at the edge of a cliff, gazing out at a swirling sea of colors. "These dreams are beautiful."

"Beauty can hide danger," Orion replied, his voice low as he scanned the room. "Stay vigilant. The shadows here can be deceptive."

As they moved deeper into the sanctuary, Lira felt a pull in her chest, a strange connection to the dreams that lingered in the air. Each step seemed to awaken the remnants of lost aspirations, fears, and desires that echoed through the stone.

Suddenly, a chilling breeze swept through the sanctuary, extinguishing the candles and plunging the room into darkness. Lira's heart raced, and she instinctively reached for Orion's hand, seeking comfort in the presence of her companion.

"Stay close," he whispered, his grip reassuring. "We need to find the dream essence before the shadows awaken."

A low growl reverberated from the darkness, sending shivers down Lira's spine. The air crackled with tension as shadowy figures emerged, swirling around them like smoke. Lira squinted, trying to make out their forms, but they shifted and twisted, evading her gaze.

"Who dares enter the realm of lost dreams?" a voice boomed, echoing off the sanctuary walls.

"I am Lira, a dreamweaver," she called out, her voice steadier than she felt. "We seek the lost dreams and the heart of the goddess."

A shadow detached from the others, taking on the form of a tall figure draped in flowing robes. Its eyes glimmered like shards of obsidian, and Lira felt a pull toward them, a deep sense of familiarity.

"The heart of the goddess?" the figure mused, tilting its head. "Many have come seeking it, yet few return. What makes you think you will succeed?"

"We're not afraid," Orion said, stepping forward. "We have to stop the nightmares from spreading. We believe the heart fragments will help restore balance to the dream realm."

The figure regarded them with an inscrutable expression. "Bravery is commendable, but the darkness is cunning. To find the heart, you must first face your own fears."

Lira's breath hitched. "What do you mean?"

"The dreams of this sanctuary are twisted reflections of those who seek them," the figure explained. "To reclaim what is lost, you must confront the shadows within your own hearts."

Before Lira could respond, the figure raised a hand, and the shadows around them swirled, transforming into swirling images—visions of their deepest fears.

Lira found herself standing alone in a vast, empty void, the darkness closing in around her. Flickering images of her nightmares emerged: the shadowy figures that haunted her sleep, their laughter echoing in her ears, urging her to forget. She stumbled backward, panic rising in her chest.

"No!" she cried, trying to push the images away. "I won't let you control me!"

Suddenly, Orion appeared beside her, his presence a steady anchor in the storm of her fears. "Lira, remember who you are. You are a dreamweaver. You have the power to shape these shadows."

Lira focused on his words, drawing strength from his unwavering support. She raised her hands, envisioning light pouring from within her, pushing against the darkness. With a determined shout, she wove the essence of her courage into the void, transforming the shadows into shimmering motes of light.

The laughter faded, replaced by a gentle hum of harmony, as the void dissolved into a radiant dreamscape filled with vibrant colors. Lira turned to Orion, relief flooding her heart. "We did it!"

Orion smiled, pride lighting up his features. "Together."

But their victory was short-lived. The shadowy figure from before re-emerged, its expression unreadable. "You have faced your fears, but this is only the beginning. The true test lies ahead."

The shadows around them began to shift again, revealing a pathway illuminated by soft, ethereal light. "Follow the path and find the essence that binds the dreams together. It will lead you to the first heart fragment, but beware—the darkness will not give up easily."

With renewed determination, Lira and Orion stepped onto the path, their hearts racing with anticipation and uncertainty. As they journeyed deeper into the sanctuary, Lira couldn't shake the feeling that their destinies were entwined, woven into the very fabric of the dreams they sought to reclaim.

"What if we fail?" Lira asked quietly, glancing at Orion.

He looked at her, his eyes shining with conviction. "We won't fail. We're meant to do this together. Besides, I believe in you, Lira."

Her heart fluttered at his words, and she felt a warmth spread through her chest. In that moment, she realized that this journey was about more than just finding the heart fragment; it was about discovering who she truly was—and the undeniable connection she shared with the enigmatic guardian at her side.

As they continued along the illuminated path, Lira couldn't help but feel that their adventure was only just beginning—a tale woven from dreams, courage, and the promise of something deeper waiting to unfold.

4

The Essence of Dreams

The luminous path twisted and turned, guiding Lira and Orion deeper into the heart of the Dreamweaver's Sanctuary. Each step resonated with an ethereal hum, vibrating with the energy of lost dreams and forgotten hopes. Lira felt a growing sense of purpose, a feeling that she was on the brink of something extraordinary.

As they walked, the shadows receded, revealing shimmering doorways adorned with intricate patterns that danced with colors. Each doorway seemed to pulse with a unique essence, drawing Lira's gaze like a magnet.

"Look at these," she murmured, her fingers brushing against the cool stone. "I can feel the dreams behind them. They're alive!"Orion nodded, his eyes reflecting the wonder she felt. "Each essence is tied to a different dreamer, a fragment of their hopes and fears. If we can harness them, they may guide us to the heart fragment we seek."

Taking a deep breath, Lira stepped toward the first doorway, its surface glistening like liquid silver. As she reached out, the door swung open, revealing a swirling vortex of color and light. With a mixture of excitement and trepidation, she stepped inside.

The world around her transformed in an instant. She found herself standing in a lush meadow bathed in golden sunlight. Vibrant flowers swayed gently in the breeze, and the air was thick with the sweet fragrance of blooming blossoms. It was a dreamscape of pure joy.

"Welcome, dreamweaver," a melodic voice chimed from behind her.

Lira turned to see a figure emerging from the flowers—a young girl with laughter in her eyes and hair like spun gold. "I am Aina, the Dreamkeeper of this essence. You've come to gather the dreams, haven't you?"

"Yes," Lira replied, awe filling her voice. "We're looking for the heart fragment of the goddess."

Aina's expression turned serious. "The heart is fragile, but it can be mended with the right essence. To find it, you must first understand the power of joy and the role it plays in the dreams of others."

Lira looked around, sensing the happiness enveloping her. "What do you mean?"

"Joy is a powerful force," Aina explained, her voice soft yet resolute. "It can illuminate the darkest corners of the heart. But it must be shared, not hoarded. Show me your joy, and I will grant you the essence you seek."

Lira hesitated, uncertainty creeping in. She had always felt joy in fleeting moments, but could she truly express it in front of a stranger? "How do I do that?"

"Close your eyes and remember," Aina encouraged. "Recall a moment when your heart soared, when laughter filled your soul. Let that memory guide you."

Taking a deep breath, Lira shut her eyes and searched her mind for a moment of pure joy. She thought of the times spent in the guild, the camaraderie of her fellow apprentices, the excitement of weaving dreams under the guidance of Master Aelion. The memory blossomed within her, filling her with warmth.

Lira opened her eyes, and a radiant smile spread across her face. "I remember a day when we all worked together to create a dream for a child in the village. His laughter echoed through the hall, and it felt like we were all part of something beautiful."

As she spoke, a soft light enveloped her, pulsating with the rhythm of her heartbeat. Aina beamed, the energy in the meadow shifting as the flowers seemed to respond, blooming even brighter.

"Now, release that joy," Aina urged. "Let it flow."

With a surge of confidence, Lira raised her hands, channeling her joy into the essence that surrounded her. Threads of light coalesced in the air, forming a shimmering orb that danced with color. The orb expanded, illuminating the meadow, and Lira felt the essence of joy intertwining with her own spirit.

Aina clapped her hands, laughter ringing like chimes in the breeze. "You have done it! You've shared your joy, and now the essence of this dream is yours."

The orb of light floated toward Lira, settling gently in her hands. She marveled at its beauty, feeling its warmth radiate through her fingers. This essence was a tangible reminder of the power of joy—a light that could pierce the darkness.

"Thank you, Aina," Lira said, her heart brimming with gratitude. "I won't forget this."

As she prepared to step back through the doorway, she felt a tug at her heart. "Wait! You must also learn to embrace sorrow," Aina said, her expression turning solemn. "The path to the heart fragment is not just about joy; it is also about understanding the depths of despair. Only then can you find true balance."

Lira nodded, understanding the weight of Aina's words. She stepped back into the sanctuary, holding the essence tightly. The shadows swirled around her, waiting expectantly.

Orion stood nearby, his eyes wide with curiosity. "What did you find?"

Lira held up the orb, its light flickering like a heartbeat. "Joy. It's powerful, and it can illuminate even the darkest dreams."

Orion smiled, a flicker of pride in his gaze. "That's a great start. But we need to find the next essence quickly. The darkness is closing in."

Without hesitating, they moved toward the next doorway, where another essence awaited them. Lira felt a mix of excitement and anxiety, knowing they would have to confront the deeper emotions that lay hidden within the shadows.

As she stepped through the second doorway, she felt a shiver run down her spine. The landscape shifted again, this time transforming into a desolate wasteland, a stark contrast to the vibrant meadow they had just left. The air was heavy with despair, and the ground was cracked and dry.

In the center of the wasteland stood a figure cloaked in darkness, its presence almost suffocating. Lira's heart raced as she recognized the embodiment of sorrow—a reflection of the pain she had buried deep within herself.

"You have entered my realm," the figure intoned, its voice echoing like thunder. "What do you seek here?"

Lira swallowed hard, determination coursing through her veins. "We're looking for the essence of sorrow. We need it to find the heart fragment."

The figure loomed closer, shrouded in shadows. "To find it, you must confront your own sorrow. Only then will you understand its power."

Lira glanced at Orion, who nodded encouragingly. She knew what she had to do. Taking a deep breath, she stepped forward, ready to face the shadows of her past.

As she stood before the embodiment of sorrow, memories flooded her mind—the loneliness of her childhood, the pain of loss, and the shadows that haunted her dreams. Tears stung her eyes as she relived those moments, each one a heavy weight upon her heart.

But just as the sorrow threatened to consume her, she felt Orion's presence beside her, his warmth dispelling the chill. "You're not alone," he whispered, his voice a soft anchor amidst the turmoil. "You're stronger than your pain."

Lira took a step back, focusing on his words. "I won't let sorrow define me. I'll transform it into strength."

With renewed resolve, she embraced her sorrow, letting the tears flow. The shadows began to shift, forming tendrils of darkness that twisted and turned around her. She raised her hands, channeling her pain into the essence that swirled around her.

A brilliant light burst forth, illuminating the wasteland and revealing the beauty hidden within sorrow. It transformed into a radiant orb that glowed with a soft, warm light, illuminating the desolation around them.

As Lira's tears mingled with the light, she felt a profound release. The shadows receded, revealing the beauty buried beneath the sorrow—a landscape awakening from its desolation, flowers blooming in defiance of despair. The orb pulsed in her hands, resonating with the power of sorrow transformed into strength.

The cloaked figure observed, its expression inscrutable. "You have embraced your sorrow and found strength in it. This is the true essence of sorrow—a reminder that even in the darkest times, there is beauty to be found. It is a necessary part of the tapestry of dreams."

Lira nodded, her heart swelling with a mixture of relief and gratitude. "Thank you for helping me understand. I didn't realize that sorrow could be a source of strength."The figure extended a hand, and the orb floated toward Lira, settling in her palm. "Take this essence. It will guide you in your quest for the heart fragment. Remember, it is through the balance of joy and sorrow that you will find the truth."

As Lira stepped back through the doorway, she felt invigorated, the weight of her emotions transformed into something powerful and illuminating. Orion was waiting, a proud smile on his face.

"You did it, Lira!" he exclaimed, glancing at the two glowing orbs in her hands. "We have joy and sorrow. Together, they will lead us closer to the heart fragment."

"Let's find the last essence," Lira replied, her spirit alight with purpose. "I feel it calling to us."

They approached the final doorway, its surface shimmering with a deep, rich hue that seemed to pulse with a heartbeat of its own. Lira's heart raced with anticipation and anxiety. What would they encounter this time?

As she pushed the door open, they were enveloped in a warm glow, finding themselves in a vast, endless sky filled with swirling clouds of vibrant colors. Below them lay a city made of crystalline towers, each one reflecting the light of the sun like prisms. The beauty was overwhelming, yet Lira felt a strange sense of unease in the air.

"Welcome, seekers," a voice rang out, echoing through the sky. From the clouds descended a figure cloaked in radiant light, their form shifting like the sunbeams breaking through the clouds. "I am Solara, the Dreamkeeper of hope."

Lira and Orion exchanged glances, awe written across their faces. "We are searching for the heart fragment of the goddess," Lira stated, her voice steady despite her nerves. "We have gathered the essences of joy and sorrow, and we need the essence of hope."

Solara smiled, their expression warm and inviting. "Hope is the bridge between despair and joy. It ignites the spark within us when we feel lost. To gather this essence, you must demonstrate your own hope—show me that you believe in a future free of darkness."

Lira felt a rush of determination. "I believe that we can restore balance to the dream realm and heal the hearts of those affected by the nightmares."

"Speak your hope into the light," Solara urged, gesturing to the swirling clouds. "Let it take form."

Lira closed her eyes, focusing on her vision of a world where dreams flourished, where joy triumphed over despair, and where the darkness was kept at bay. She imagined children laughing in the sunlight, villagers sharing their dreams, and the goddess smiling down upon them.

"I hope for a world where dreams can thrive without fear," she spoke, her voice ringing with conviction. "A world where we can weave our dreams together, supporting one another against the darkness."

As her words left her lips, a bright light erupted from her heart, expanding into the air around her. It filled the sky with colors more vibrant than she had ever seen, illuminating the clouds with hope. The swirling colors took the shape of butterflies, each one representing a dream or a wish waiting to be fulfilled.

Solara watched in awe, their eyes reflecting the brilliance of Lira's hope. "You have shown me the essence of hope, dreamweaver. You understand that hope is not simply wishful thinking; it is the courage to believe in a better tomorrow."

The butterflies danced around Lira and Orion, showering them with sparkling light. From this shimmering display, an orb of brilliant hope emerged, floating gracefully into Lira's outstretched hands.

"Take this essence, and may it guide you in your quest," Solara said, their voice filled with warmth and wisdom. "Remember, hope can light the way through even the darkest of nights."

As the orb settled next to the others, Lira felt a profound sense of completeness. They had gathered the three essences—joy, sorrow, and hope—and with them, the power to heal and restore the dream realm.

"Thank you, Solara," Lira said, her heart brimming with gratitude. "We won't let this hope fade."

With the essences in hand, she and Orion made their way back through the door, ready to confront the darkness and reclaim the heart fragment of the goddess.As they returned to the sanctuary, the shadows shifted and churned, a palpable tension hanging in the air. Lira could feel the darkness closing in, waiting for an opportunity to strike.

"It's time," Orion said, determination etched on his face. "We need to use the essences to confront the shadows and find the heart fragment before it's too late."

Lira nodded, her resolve solidifying. They would face the darkness together, armed with the power of their emotions—joy, sorrow, and hope.

As they stepped forward, the shadows writhed, and the cloaked figure reappeared, its obsidian eyes gleaming with malevolence. "You think you can reclaim what was lost?" it taunted, voice dripping with disdain. "You are but a flicker of light in a world consumed by darkness."

"We are more than a flicker," Lira declared, holding the orbs high. "We carry the essences of joy, sorrow, and hope. We will restore balance to the dream realm!"

The shadows surged, but Lira and Orion stood firm. Drawing upon the essences, they wove their energy together, merging the light into a brilliant tapestry of color. As they channeled the combined power, the darkness recoiled, shrieking as the light intensified.

"Together!" Orion urged, and Lira nodded, feeling the strength of their connection.

With a final burst of energy, they unleashed the essence, sending a wave of light crashing into the shadows. The darkness writhed and twisted, but the radiant light pierced through, illuminating the sanctuary.

In that moment, Lira felt an incredible surge of power, a deep connection to the dreams that had come before them and those that were yet to come. She could sense the goddess's heart calling to her, guiding her toward the truth.

As the shadows began to dissipate, a pulsing light emerged from the heart of the sanctuary—a fragment of the goddess's heart, glowing with vibrant energy. It floated toward Lira and Orion, radiating warmth and light."Together, we can reclaim what was lost," Lira whispered, her heart pounding with anticipation. They had faced the darkness and emerged stronger, united in their purpose.

The fragment settled in Lira's hands, its energy intertwining with the essences they had gathered. "Now we must restore the heart," Orion said, his voice steady.

Lira nodded, determination filling her soul. With the power of their emotions and the heart fragment, they would heal the dream realm and protect it from the darkness.

Together, they would forge a new destiny, one where dreams could thrive, unshackled by fear—a destiny that echoed with the promise of love, courage, and hope.

5

The Heart of the Dream

The pulsing heart fragment thrummed in Lira's hands, radiating warmth and light that washed over her like a gentle tide. As she held it, a vision unfolded in her mind—a vivid tapestry of dreams, hopes, and sorrows interwoven into a singular thread, binding the realm of dreams together.

"This is it," Lira breathed, her heart racing. "The goddess's heart."

Orion nodded, his expression a mix of awe and determination. "We need to restore it to its rightful place. It's the key to bringing balance back to the dream realm."

They stood at the center of the Dreamweaver's Sanctuary, the echoes of their triumph still resonating in the air. But with the darkness momentarily at bay, Lira felt a sense of urgency. Time was of the essence, and the heart fragment pulsed in a rhythm that matched her racing heartbeat.

"Where do we place it?" Lira asked, scanning the sanctuary for any sign of a suitable location.

"The altar," Orion suggested, pointing to a raised platform adorned with intricate carvings of dreams and nightmares. "That must be where the heart belongs."

With newfound purpose, they made their way to the altar, the heart fragment glowing brighter with each step they took. The sanctuary was alive with energy, the walls whispering secrets and ancient truths as they approached the pedestal.

As they reached the altar, Lira felt a deep connection to the space around her, as if the dreams of countless dreamers were beckoning her forward. She placed the heart fragment gently on the altar, and a brilliant light erupted, filling the sanctuary with an overwhelming radiance.

In that moment, the heart fragment melded seamlessly into the altar, a perfect union of light and energy. Lira closed her eyes, allowing the warmth to envelop her, and she felt the essence of joy, sorrow, and hope intertwining within her.

"Now what?" Orion asked, glancing around nervously as the sanctuary hummed with anticipation.

Lira opened her eyes, her gaze fixed on the altar. "I think we need to channel our energy into it. We have to invoke the essence of the goddess and awaken her spirit."

Orion nodded, determination set in his features. "Let's do it."

They stood side by side, hands outstretched toward the heart on the altar. Lira focused on the essences they had gathered, feeling their combined power surge through her veins. She thought of the laughter of children, the tears of sorrow transformed into strength, and the flickering flame of hope that guided them through darkness.

"Goddess of Dreams, hear us!" Lira called out, her voice strong and unwavering. "We bring forth the essence of joy, sorrow, and hope to restore your heart and heal the dream realm!"

The light from the heart intensified, swirling around them in a whirlwind of color and sound. Lira felt herself being lifted, as if the energy was carrying her higher into the realm of dreams. Beside her, Orion steadied himself, their connection unwavering.

Suddenly, a voice echoed through the sanctuary—a melodic tone that resonated with ancient wisdom and power. "Children of dreams, you have summoned me."

Lira gasped as the light coalesced into a shimmering figure, the goddess emerging from the brilliance like a radiant star. She was ethereal, her form shifting with the hues of dawn, her eyes reflecting the boundless skies.

"Goddess," Lira breathed, awe washing over her. "We've come to restore your heart and bring balance back to the dream realm."

The goddess smiled, her presence filling the sanctuary with warmth. "Your journey has been arduous, yet you have shown great courage and resilience. You have gathered the essences of joy, sorrow, and hope, and through your unity, you have revived my heart."

Lira felt a swell of emotion, her heart swelling with pride. "We couldn't have done it without each other. We realized that all emotions, even the painful ones, are part of the tapestry of dreams."

The goddess nodded, her gaze piercing into Lira's soul. "You understand the truth that binds us all. The dream realm flourishes when its inhabitants embrace their emotions, for it is through them that dreams take flight."

Orion stepped forward, his voice steady. "What can we do to protect the dream realm from the darkness that seeks to consume it?"

The goddess's expression turned serious. "The shadows that threaten to engulf the dreams arise from fear and despair. You must continue to cultivate joy, share sorrow, and nurture hope among the dreamers. Only then can you create a shield against the encroaching darkness."

Lira felt a surge of determination. "We'll spread the essences throughout the dream realm. We won't let fear take hold."

With a wave of her hand, the goddess beckoned them closer. "Take this," she said, extending a radiant orb of light—a fragment of her own essence. "It will guide you in your quest to spread joy, sorrow, and hope to those who have lost their way. Protect it, for it is a beacon for dreamers."

Lira reached out, accepting the orb, feeling its warmth seep into her skin, filling her with power and purpose. "Thank you, goddess. We won't let you down."

As the goddess's presence began to fade, she imparted one final piece of wisdom. "Remember, the strength of dreams lies within the hearts of those who dare to dream. Trust in one another, for you are stronger together."

With those words echoing in their minds, the sanctuary began to dissolve, the brilliance of the goddess enveloping them as they were pulled back into the waking world.

Lira and Orion landed softly on the grassy hill where their adventure had begun, the sun setting on the horizon. The air was thick with the scent of wildflowers, and the warmth of the goddess's light still lingered around them.

"We did it," Orion said, disbelief mingling with joy in his voice. "We actually brought her back!"

Lira clutched the orb tightly, a smile spreading across her face. "Now, we need to spread her message. We have to find the dreamers who need our help."

As they stood together, the weight of their journey settling over them, Lira realized how much they had grown. They were no longer just apprentices; they were protectors of dreams, bound by a shared purpose and the promise of a brighter tomorrow.

"Let's start in the village," Lira suggested, her determination renewed. "There are so many who need to hear the message of hope and healing."

With that, they began their descent down the hill, ready to face whatever challenges awaited them. Lira felt a sense of unity with Orion, a bond forged in the fires of their shared adventure. As they walked, the warmth of the orb in her hand pulsed gently, a reminder of the journey ahead.

But in the distance, a shadow flickered, a reminder that their path would not be without obstacles. The darkness they had faced still loomed, and Lira knew they must remain vigilant.

"Together, we'll shine a light against the darkness," Lira vowed, glancing at Orion. "We'll make sure that dreams can flourish."

"Together," Orion echoed, determination blazing in his eyes.

And with that, they ventured forth into the twilight, the promise of new adventures waiting just beyond the horizon.

6

Whispers of the Night

As Lira and Orion made their way down the hill, the fading sunlight painted the sky with hues of orange and purple, casting a warm glow over the landscape. The village lay nestled in the valley below, a cluster of homes with chimneys puffing soft clouds of smoke into the twilight. Lira felt a surge of hope at the thought of sharing the goddess's message, but a knot of unease lingered in her stomach. They had triumphed over darkness, yet it still lurked on the edges of their reality.

"We need to gather the villagers," Lira said, her voice steady despite her nerves. "They must know that the heart of the goddess is restored and that there's hope for the dream realm."

"Let's start at the tavern," Orion suggested. "It's usually the heart of the village, where people gather to share stories and news."

As they approached the tavern, the sound of laughter and music floated through the open windows. The atmosphere buzzed with life, but Lira couldn't shake the feeling that the villagers were unaware of the darkness threatening their dreams. She took a deep breath, steeling herself for what was to come.

Inside, the tavern was warm and inviting, with wooden beams overhead and flickering candlelight casting soft shadows on the walls. Villagers filled the space, their voices mingling in a chorus of excitement and camaraderie. Lira spotted familiar faces—friends, neighbors, and children—all caught up in their own world, oblivious to the encroaching shadows.

"Lira! Orion!" called out Anya, a bright-eyed girl from the village, waving them over. "Come join us!"

Lira exchanged a glance with Orion, who nodded encouragingly. They made their way to the table, where Anya sat with a group of friends, their laughter infectious.

"What brings you two here?" Anya asked, her curiosity evident. "You've been gone for so long!"

"We have important news," Lira began, feeling the weight of her words. "The heart of the goddess has been restored, and we need your help to spread hope throughout the village."

The table quieted, and the air grew heavy with anticipation. "What do you mean?" a boy named Rian asked, leaning forward. "What happened?"

Lira took a deep breath, gathering her thoughts. "We journeyed through the dream realm, faced darkness, and discovered the essences of joy, sorrow, and hope. The goddess's heart was broken, but we managed to restore it, and now we have a message to share."

Orion chimed in, "We need to come together as a community. We must remind each other that even in darkness, we can find light. We can help those who've lost hope."

Anya's eyes sparkled with excitement. "That's amazing! But how can we help?"

Lira smiled, feeling the warmth of camaraderie fill the space. "We can create a festival, a gathering where everyone shares their dreams and stories. We'll invite the entire village to celebrate hope and healing."

The villagers exchanged glances, their expressions shifting from curiosity to enthusiasm. "We can share songs, tell stories, and dance," Rian suggested, a grin spreading across his face. "It will be a festival of dreams!"

Lira's heart soared. "Yes! We can gather all the villagers and remind them of the beauty in their dreams. Together, we'll weave a tapestry of hope!"

As the villagers rallied around the idea, Lira felt the knot of unease in her stomach begin to dissolve. This was what they needed—a way to connect, to share their emotions, and to stand together against the darkness that threatened to consume their dreams.

The energy in the tavern shifted, laughter and excitement bubbling up once more. Lira and Orion joined in the discussions, planning the details of the festival, from the decorations to the food and music. The villagers were invigorated, united in a common purpose.

However, as they made plans, a shadow flickered at the edge of Lira's vision. She glanced toward the window, the fading light casting long shadows across the tavern. The feeling of unease crept back in, and she couldn't shake the sensation that something was watching them.

"Are you sure everything is okay?" Orion asked, noticing Lira's sudden shift in demeanor. "You seem a bit distracted."

"I just have this feeling," Lira replied, her brow furrowed. "Like something is lurking in the shadows, waiting for us to let our guard down."

Orion glanced toward the window but saw only the gentle glow of the evening sky. "Maybe it's just the remnants of our journey. We've been through a lot."

"Perhaps," Lira said, but the unease lingered. "I just want to make sure the festival is a safe space for everyone."

As the plans for the festival continued to unfold, Lira's mind remained partially occupied with the lingering sense of foreboding. The villagers began to gather supplies, gathering flowers, weaving garlands, and preparing for the celebration of hope and healing.

The tavern buzzed with energy, and as night fell, lanterns were lit, casting a warm glow that enveloped the room. Lira and Orion worked alongside the villagers, the excitement contagious, but each flicker of light reminded Lira of the shadows lurking just beyond their reach.

As they stepped outside to gather more flowers, Lira turned to Orion, her voice low. "I can't shake this feeling that the darkness isn't finished with us yet. What if it tries to disrupt the festival?"

Orion's expression hardened with resolve. "Then we'll face it together. We've faced darkness before, and we can do it again. But first, we need to focus on bringing everyone together for the festival."

Lira nodded, feeling reassured by his words, but the weight of the unknown still pressed on her heart. They continued to gather flowers under the watchful eye of the stars, the night air thick with anticipation.

As they returned to the tavern, laughter and music filled the air, creating a comforting backdrop. Lira noticed a group of children playing nearby, their joy infectious. She couldn't help but smile, feeling a flicker of hope amidst her worries.

Just then, the door of the tavern swung open, and a gust of wind swept through the room, carrying with it a chill that seemed to silence the laughter. Lira shivered and instinctively stepped closer to Orion.

"Did anyone else feel that?" she asked, glancing around.

The villagers exchanged nervous looks, the atmosphere shifting from joyous to tense. Anya stepped forward, her brow furrowed. "What was that?"

Suddenly, a voice broke through the tension—a low, mocking laugh that sent a shiver down Lira's spine. "Oh, how quaint. A festival of hope. Do you truly believe you can banish the darkness with a few songs and tales?"

A figure emerged from the shadows, cloaked in a swirling mass of blackness. Its eyes glowed like embers, piercing through the darkness. The air grew heavy with an oppressive energy, and Lira felt her heart race.

"Who are you?" Lira demanded, trying to sound brave despite the fear gripping her.

"I am the Shade, the embodiment of fear and despair," the figure said, its voice dripping with disdain. "You've awakened the heart of the goddess, but do you think you can protect the dream realm from me? Hope is a fragile thing, easily extinguished."

Lira stepped forward, her fists clenched. "We won't let you destroy what we've built. We're stronger together!"

The Shade let out a chilling laugh, the sound reverberating through the tavern. "Stronger together? How amusing. I thrive on fear, and I can sense your doubts. You think you can shield the villagers from me? I will show you the true meaning of despair."

Orion stepped protectively in front of Lira, his expression fierce. "You won't take anyone from us. We've faced darkness before, and we won't back down now."

The Shade's laughter echoed in the night, and with a wave of its hand, shadows coiled around the villagers, pulling them into a swirling mass of darkness. Panic erupted in the tavern as people scrambled to escape the encroaching shadows.

"Lira!" Orion shouted, his voice strained. "We need to focus! Use the essences!"

Lira felt the warmth of the orb in her hand, its light flickering against the oppressive darkness. "Everyone, listen!" she called out, her voice rising above the chaos. "We have joy, sorrow, and hope! We can't let fear take hold!"

As she spoke, Lira closed her eyes and drew upon the energy of the essences. She envisioned the light of joy filling the room, the strength of sorrow transforming into resilience, and the flickering flame of hope illuminating the shadows.

"Together!" she urged, reaching out to Orion and the villagers. "We must channel our emotions into the light! Embrace your dreams!"

With a shared breath, the villagers focused their thoughts, the warmth of their dreams swirling around them. Lira felt the essences rise, weaving through the air like ribbons of light, pushing back against the darkness.

The Shade hissed in frustration as the light began to push back the shadows. "You think this will stop me? You're only delaying the inevitable!"

But Lira felt the collective strength of the villagers, their dreams and hopes merging with her own. "No!" she cried, her voice unwavering. "Together, we can stand against you!"

With a surge of energy, they unleashed the combined power of joy, sorrow, and hope, creating a radiant wave of light that surged forward, pushing back the shadows and illuminating the tavern with brilliant colors.

The Shade recoiled, its form flickering as it struggled against the onslaught of light. "This isn't over!" it shrieked, its voice a blend of rage and fear.

"Leave this place!" Lira shouted, her heart pounding with determination. "You will not take our dreams!"

With one final burst of energy, the light enveloped the Shade, forcing it into the depths of the night. The darkness writhed, then shattered into a thousand shards, dissolving into the air like mist.

As the last remnants of the Shade vanished, the villagers erupted into cheers, their spirits lifted as the oppressive energy dissipated. Lira felt the warmth of the orb pulsing in her hand, a reminder of their collective strength.

"We did it!" Anya exclaimed, her eyes shining with excitement. "We pushed it back!"

Orion turned to Lira, a mixture of pride and concern etched on his face. "But it won't stop there. We need to remain vigilant. The darkness will always seek to return."

Lira nodded, her heart still racing. "We'll protect our dreams. Together, we can face whatever comes next."

As the villagers celebrated their victory, Lira felt a renewed sense of purpose. The festival would still happen, but now it would be a celebration of resilience—a testament to the strength of their dreams against the darkness.

And in that moment, she realized that as long as they held onto their hope, they could overcome anything. The dream realm would thrive, and together, they would continue to weave a tapestry of light in a world threatened by shadows.

7
The Festival of Dreams

The dawn of the festival arrived, bathing the village in golden light. Lira awoke with a sense of purpose coursing through her veins. The remnants of the Shade's darkness still lingered in her mind, but the excitement of the festival pushed those thoughts aside. Today would be a celebration—a reaffirmation of hope and resilience.

As she stepped outside, the crisp morning air filled her lungs, invigorating her spirit. The village was alive with activity. Colorful banners fluttered in the gentle breeze, and the aroma of baked goods wafted through the streets. Villagers adorned in vibrant clothing buzzed with anticipation, laughter ringing out as they prepared for the day's festivities.

"Lira!" Anya called, running up to her, her cheeks flushed with excitement. "We're almost ready! The decorations look amazing!"

Lira smiled, her heart swelling with joy. "I can't believe how much everyone has come together for this. It's incredible!"

Anya nodded vigorously. "We'll have games, storytelling, dancing—everything! It'll be the best festival ever!"

As they walked through the village, Lira could see the impact of their collective energy. Children were weaving flowers into garlands, while others painted vibrant murals depicting dreams. The tavern had transformed into a hub of creativity, filled with painted stones and drawings of fantastical creatures.

"We'll gather everyone in the square to begin," Anya said, her eyes shining with determination. "It's important to remind everyone of the heart of the goddess and the power of our dreams."

Lira felt a thrill at the thought of sharing the essence of joy, sorrow, and hope with the villagers. "Let's do it. We'll inspire them to embrace their dreams!"

As the sun climbed higher, the villagers began to gather in the square, their faces alight with excitement. Lira took her place at the center, feeling the weight of their hopes and fears resting on her shoulders.

"Welcome, everyone!" she called, her voice ringing through the air. "Today, we celebrate the Festival of Dreams, a day to honor the heart of the goddess and to share our stories, our dreams, and our hopes!"

The crowd cheered, the sound reverberating through the square. Lira's heart swelled with pride as she looked out at her friends, family, and neighbors—all united in purpose.

"Let us remember," she continued, "that even in the darkest times, we can find strength in one another. The heart of the goddess has been restored, and through our unity, we can push back the shadows that seek to consume us."

Orion stepped forward, his presence steady beside her. "Today, we will share our dreams and remind each other of the light that lives within us all. Let's celebrate the beauty of our hopes!"

With a wave of her hand, Lira signaled the start of the festivities. Children dashed off to participate in games, while musicians began to play cheerful melodies. Laughter echoed in the square as people joined together to dance, their movements flowing in harmony with the music.

Lira and Orion mingled with the crowd, encouraging villagers to share their dreams. They listened to stories of love, adventure, and bravery, each tale adding to the tapestry of hope they were weaving together.

As the sun began to dip in the sky, painting everything in hues of pink and gold, Lira felt a moment of quiet amidst the chaos. She stepped away from the festivities for a moment, seeking solace near the edge of the square.

But as she took a deep breath, the sense of foreboding returned. The shadows of the Shade lingered in her mind, a reminder that the darkness could return at any moment. She closed her eyes, willing herself to focus on the warmth of the light around her, the laughter and joy that filled the air.

"Lira?" Orion's voice broke through her thoughts, grounding her in the moment. "Are you okay?"

She opened her eyes, forcing a smile. "Yeah, just taking it all in. It feels incredible, doesn't it?"

Orion nodded, but concern flickered in his eyes. "I know we've pushed back the darkness for now, but we have to stay vigilant. We can't let our guard down."

"I know," Lira replied, her heart heavy. "But today is a day to celebrate. We have to believe that we can protect our dreams."

As the night settled over the village, lanterns lit up the square, creating a magical ambiance. Villagers gathered around a large bonfire, its flames dancing and crackling, casting flickering shadows on their faces.

"Let's gather for stories!" Lira called, a spark of excitement igniting within her. "Share your dreams and your hopes!"

One by one, villagers stepped forward, sharing their tales of adventure and love, of loss and rebirth. Lira listened, captivated by the tapestry of emotions woven into each story. She felt the weight of their dreams and sorrows, and with each tale, her resolve grew stronger.

As the fire blazed, Lira felt a surge of energy. "Let's remember our connection to the goddess! We can channel her light and bring hope to those who need it most!"

With a nod from Orion, they encouraged the villagers to focus their thoughts on the goddess's heart, channeling their dreams and hopes into the flames. The fire pulsed with light, transforming into a brilliant spectacle that illuminated the night.

Suddenly, as the flames danced higher, a familiar voice echoed through the square, resonating with power. "Children of dreams, I am with you!"

The villagers gasped, awe washing over them as the ethereal form of the goddess appeared above the bonfire, her presence radiating warmth and light. "You have honored me with your stories and your unity. The heart of the goddess beats within each of you, and it is through your dreams that we can continue to protect the realm."

Lira's heart swelled with joy. "Thank you, goddess! We will keep your heart safe and ensure that dreams flourish!"

The goddess smiled, her eyes sparkling like stars. "Remember, the strength of dreams lies within your hearts. Together, you can overcome any darkness that seeks to invade your realm."

As her presence enveloped the square, the villagers felt a renewed sense of hope and connection. Lira looked at

Orion, their eyes meeting with a shared understanding. They were not alone in this fight; they were bound by their dreams and the promise of a brighter future.

As the goddess faded, the villagers erupted into cheers, their spirits lifted. Lira felt a sense of accomplishment, knowing they had created something beautiful—a celebration of dreams that would resonate within the village for years to come.

"Let's keep the festivities going!" Orion shouted, his voice ringing with enthusiasm.

With renewed energy, the villagers danced, sang, and shared their dreams long into the night. Lira joined in, her laughter blending with the music and joy that filled the air. In that moment, she knew they had forged a powerful bond—a unity that would stand strong against the shadows.

But as the fire crackled and the night deepened, Lira couldn't shake the feeling that the Shade's presence still lingered, waiting for the right moment to strike. They had won this battle, but the war against the darkness was far from over.

As she danced under the stars, she resolved to remain vigilant. Together with Orion and the villagers, they would keep the light of hope burning bright, ensuring that their dreams could thrive no matter the challenges ahead.

8
Echoes of the Past

The festival continued into the night, with laughter and music echoing through the village. As the stars twinkled above, Lira found herself caught up in the joy of the moment, yet the shadow of unease remained nestled in her heart. She couldn't shake the feeling that the darkness was not yet vanquished.

"Lira!" Anya called, her voice filled with excitement as she approached with a group of children. "We're about to start the storytelling circle! You have to join us!"

Lira smiled, grateful for the distraction. "Of course! I'd love to hear everyone's stories."

As they gathered around the bonfire, the flickering flames illuminated the eager faces of the children. Lira settled beside Orion, who gave her a reassuring smile. The warmth of the fire felt comforting against the cool night air.

Anya took the lead, her eyes sparkling with enthusiasm. "Let's begin with the tale of the Dreamweaver! Who wants to share?"

A young boy named Kiran stood up, puffing out his chest. "I'll go first! The Dreamweaver is a magical being who weaves the dreams of all creatures into the fabric of the night. One day, she discovered that darkness had begun to consume the dreams, and she knew she had to save them!"

The group leaned in closer, captivated by Kiran's animated storytelling. He continued, describing how the Dreamweaver ventured into the shadowy realm, gathering fragments of light and hope to restore balance to the dream world. The children listened intently, their eyes wide with wonder.

After Kiran finished, applause erupted from the circle. Lira felt her heart swell with pride at the creativity blooming around the fire. One by one, each child shared their tales of adventure, bravery, and hope, weaving a rich tapestry of stories that filled the night.

As the tales unfolded, Lira felt an overwhelming sense of belonging. This community, united by dreams, had become her family. The worries that had plagued her since the encounter with the Shade began to fade, replaced by the warmth of shared experiences.

But as the last story concluded and the crowd erupted into cheers, a chill ran down Lira's spine. She glanced toward the edge of the square, where the shadows seemed to flicker unnaturally. The flickering flames cast a veil of uncertainty over the joyous celebration.

"Orion," she whispered, her voice laced with concern. "Do you see that?"

He turned, his expression shifting from joy to alertness. "Yeah. The shadows... they look different. Almost alive."

Before they could react, a cold wind swept through the square, extinguishing a few nearby lanterns and causing the flames of the bonfire to flicker violently. The laughter of the villagers dimmed, replaced by a tense silence.

From the darkness, a figure emerged—a tall, cloaked shadow with glowing eyes that pierced through the night.

Lira's heart raced as recognition set in.

"The Shade!" she gasped, stepping protectively in front of the children.

"You thought you could celebrate without consequence?" the Shade's voice echoed, dripping with malice. "Hope is a fragile illusion, easily shattered."

Lira clenched her fists, her pulse pounding in her ears. "We won't let you take our joy! You're not welcome here!"

The Shade let out a chilling laugh, the sound reverberating through the square. "Joy? You think you can shield yourselves with stories and songs? I thrive in fear and despair!"

"Not if we stand together!" Orion shouted, his voice steady despite the encroaching darkness.

The villagers began to murmur anxiously, fear creeping into their hearts as they realized the Shade had returned. Lira felt the collective dread but also the flicker of determination igniting among her friends.

"Gather your strength!" Lira urged the villagers. "Remember the light within you! We have the heart of the goddess!"

With a nod from Orion, Lira focused on the warmth radiating from the orb in her pocket. It pulsed gently, reminding her of the essences they had restored. "We need to channel our dreams—our hopes—together!"

As the villagers began to chant, Lira closed her eyes, drawing on the memories of the festival—the laughter, the stories, the sense of unity that had filled the air. She envisioned the essences swirling around them, illuminating the darkness.

"Feel the warmth of joy," she called out, her voice rising above the wind. "Embrace the strength of sorrow and the resilience of hope!"

The villagers began to chant in unison, their voices blending into a powerful melody that reverberated through the square. Lira could feel the energy rising, the essence of their collective dreams manifesting into a radiant light.

The Shade recoiled, its form flickering as the light pushed back the shadows. "This won't hold me!" it hissed, but Lira could sense its fear.

"We are not alone," Orion declared, standing tall beside her. "Our unity is stronger than your darkness!"

With a final surge of energy, Lira and the villagers directed the light toward the Shade, enveloping it in a blinding radiance. The darkness writhed and twisted, its form disintegrating under the weight of their collective strength.

"No! This isn't the end!" the Shade screamed as it vanished, leaving behind a lingering echo of its presence.

As the light subsided and the villagers looked around in disbelief, a hushed silence fell over the square. Then, slowly, a wave of relief washed over them, followed by a roar of victory.

"We did it!" Anya shouted, her voice ringing with triumph. "We pushed it back!"

Lira felt a rush of adrenaline, her heart soaring with pride. "Together, we are stronger! This is proof that we can overcome any darkness!"

But even as the villagers celebrated, Lira couldn't shake the feeling that the Shade would return. The darkness might have retreated for now, but it was still lurking in the shadows, waiting for another chance to strike.

"Orion," she murmured, her voice barely above a whisper. "What if it comes back again?"

He took her hand, squeezing it gently. "We'll be ready. We've proven that we can fight back, and we'll keep standing together. No matter what."

Lira nodded, drawing strength from his words. The festival may have been a celebration of dreams, but it had also become a testament to their resilience. They would not allow fear to dictate their lives.

As the night continued, the villagers gathered around the bonfire once more, their spirits high. Lira joined in the celebrations, but her heart remained vigilant. The fight against darkness was far from over, and they would need to prepare for whatever lay ahead.

In the warmth of the firelight and the company of her friends, Lira resolved to embrace their dreams and protect them at all costs. Together, they would face the shadows, united by their hopes and the strength they had forged in the heart of the festival.

9

A Journey of Secrets

The dawn after the festival dawned bright and clear, yet Lira awoke with a heaviness in her heart. Although the villagers had triumphed over the Shade, the feeling of unease lingered. As the echoes of the festival faded into the past, the reality of the threat still loomed ahead.

Lira sat up in bed, rubbing the sleep from her eyes, and gazed out the window. The village looked peaceful, the sun casting golden rays over the dew-kissed grass. But peace felt fragile. She could still hear the Shade's haunting voice in her mind, echoing its promise of return.

With a deep breath, she resolved to take action. If the Shade was coming back, they needed to understand more about its origins and weaknesses. They couldn't rely on the strength of dreams alone; they needed knowledge.

After breakfast, Lira sought out Orion, who was tending to the gardens near the village's edge. He noticed her approach and straightened, wiping his brow with the back of his hand. "Good morning, Lira. You seem deep in thought."

"I am," she replied, glancing back toward the village center where the festivities had taken place just the night before. "I think we need to learn more about the Shade. There might be something in the old archives or legends that can help us prepare."

Orion nodded, his expression turning serious. "You're right. We should look into the village archives. There might be texts or stories that have been passed down through generations."

The two set off toward the village library, a quaint building filled with the scent of old parchment and the weight of countless stories. Dust motes danced in the beams of sunlight streaming through the windows, and the air was thick with the promise of forgotten knowledge.

Inside, the shelves were lined with books and scrolls, some faded and worn, others pristine and untouched. Lira felt a thrill of anticipation as she stepped inside, her fingers brushing along the spines of the books.

"Where should we start?" she asked, her heart racing with the possibilities.

Orion scanned the shelves. "Let's check the section on local legends. There may be stories about the Shade and its origins."

They began to sift through the shelves, pulling down books and scrolls, flipping through pages filled with beautiful illustrations and handwritten notes. The sun moved across the sky as they searched, but time felt irrelevant as they immersed themselves in the lore of their ancestors.

Hours later, Lira stumbled upon a dusty tome bound in deep blue leather. Its title, "Whispers of the Ancients," was embossed in gold, and it seemed to hum with energy as she opened it. Within its pages were illustrations of various creatures and spirits, each accompanied by tales of their powers and weaknesses.

"Orion! Look at this!" Lira exclaimed, pointing to a page depicting a creature similar to the Shade. The drawing illustrated a dark figure surrounded by swirling shadows, with a glimmering heart encased in light.

"It says here," Lira read aloud, "that the Shade is a manifestation of despair, drawing strength from the fears of those it encounters. But it can be weakened by hope—pure, untainted hope."

"Hope as a weapon," Orion mused, leaning closer to the page. "It makes sense. We've seen how our dreams pushed it back before."

"But there's more," Lira continued, tracing her finger along the text. "The legends speak of a hidden artifact—the Heartstone of Dreams. It is said to amplify the power of hope and protect against the darkness. If we can find it, it could give us an edge against the Shade."

"Where is it located?" Orion asked, leaning forward with excitement.

Lira flipped to the next page, her heart racing. "It says here that the Heartstone is hidden in the Valley of Whispers, a place known for its ethereal beauty and perilous paths. Only those who are pure of heart can navigate its trials to retrieve the stone."

A spark of determination ignited within them. "We have to go," Lira declared, her voice steady. "If we can find the Heartstone, it might just be the key to defeating the Shade once and for all."

Orion nodded, his eyes shining with resolve. "Then we need to prepare. The valley won't be easy to traverse, and we should gather supplies and inform the others."

As they gathered their things and headed back toward the village, Lira felt a mix of excitement and trepidation. This journey could lead them to the answers they sought—or into the heart of danger.

Once back in the village, they sought out Anya and a few other trusted friends. The sun hung low in the sky, casting long shadows as they gathered in the village square, the remnants of the festival still lingering in the air.

"Everyone," Lira began, her voice steady but laced with urgency. "We've found a way to fight the Shade. There's an artifact called the Heartstone of Dreams hidden in the Valley of Whispers. We believe it can help us."

Anya's eyes widened. "The Valley of Whispers? I've heard stories about that place. It's beautiful, but dangerous."

"We know," Orion added. "But we can't allow the Shade to return. We need to retrieve the Heartstone to protect our dreams."

The villagers exchanged glances, fear mingling with determination. Lira could sense the collective anxiety but also the desire to stand strong against the darkness.

"Who will come with us?" Lira asked, her heart pounding in her chest. "We'll need a team."

"I'll go!" Anya declared, stepping forward. "We're in this together."

"Me too," Kiran added, his youthful enthusiasm infectious. "I want to help!"

One by one, others stepped forward, each expressing their willingness to join the quest. Lira felt a swell of gratitude and pride as she looked at her friends. They were united in purpose, and together, they could face whatever lay ahead.

With their team assembled, they began to gather supplies—food, water, and anything they might need for their journey. Lira felt a sense of camaraderie and purpose building as they prepared, each member contributing their unique skills and strengths.

As twilight settled over the village, Lira gathered everyone for a final meeting. "Tomorrow, we set out at dawn. Remember, the journey will test us, but we must keep our hearts focused on hope. Together, we can overcome the darkness."

The villagers nodded, their expressions resolute. Lira felt a warmth spread through her chest, the belief that they could triumph over the Shade igniting a fire within her.

That night, as Lira lay in bed, she stared at the stars through her window, wondering what awaited them in the Valley of Whispers. She thought of the Heartstone, the power it held, and the challenges they would face.

But as she closed her eyes, she also thought of her friends—Orion, Anya, Kiran, and the others—who stood beside her, their dreams intertwining with her own. Together, they would forge their path, facing whatever darkness lay ahead.

With a final deep breath, Lira drifted into sleep, her heart filled with hope for the journey that awaited them at dawn.

10
Valley of Whispers

Dawn broke with a golden light that bathed the village in warmth, but the air carried a sense of anticipation. Lira, Orion, Anya, Kiran, and the rest of their group gathered near the village gates, packs on their backs and determination in their hearts. Their journey to the Valley of Whispers was about to begin.

Lira's mind raced as they prepared to depart. The ancient texts had mentioned the Heartstone, a powerful relic that could amplify hope and push back the darkness. But the path ahead was unclear, and the Valley was known for its dangers—both natural and supernatural.

Orion approached her, his expression calm but focused. "Are you ready?"

Lira nodded, gripping the strap of her bag. "As ready as I'll ever be. But I can't shake the feeling that we're walking into something far more dangerous than we know."

Orion placed a reassuring hand on her shoulder. "We're in this together, Lira. Whatever comes, we'll face it as one." His voice was steady, and Lira found comfort in his presence. She took a deep breath, nodding again.

The group set off, leaving the familiar warmth of the village behind. The road to the Valley of Whispers was long and winding, cutting through dense forests and rugged hills. As they walked, Lira couldn't help but notice the subtle changes in the landscape—the way the wind seemed to whisper more urgently through the trees, the shadows growing deeper with each step.

Anya, always the optimist, tried to keep spirits high. "Remember, everyone," she said with a grin, "the Valley might have its dangers, but it's also said to be the most beautiful place in the realm. We'll get to see something most people only hear about in legends!"

Kiran, walking beside her, beamed. "I'm ready for adventure!"

As the hours passed, the forest became denser, the sunlight struggling to break through the thick canopy of leaves above. The group moved cautiously, aware that the path ahead would only grow more treacherous.

By midday, they stopped for a brief rest beside a clear stream, the sound of the water offering a moment of peace. Lira sat on a rock, watching as Orion filled their canteens, while Anya and Kiran splashed water on their faces.

"You're quiet," Orion remarked as he handed Lira her canteen. "What's on your mind?"

Lira took a sip of water before answering. "I'm just thinking about the Shade, and how it seemed to know more about us than we did about it. What if there's more to its connection with the Valley? What if it's drawn to the Heartstone, too?"

Orion considered her words. "That's possible. The texts didn't say much about the Heartstone's exact location or what guards it. But if the Shade is tied to despair, and the Heartstone amplifies hope, it makes sense that they're connected."

Lira's brow furrowed. "We need to stay on guard. The closer we get, the more likely it is that the Shade or something worse will try to stop us."

Just as she spoke, the wind shifted, carrying with it a low, haunting sound. The group fell silent, listening as the whispers seemed to grow louder, swirling around them in a ghostly chorus. It was as if the very air was alive with unseen voices.

"We're getting close," Anya whispered, her eyes wide with wonder. "The Valley of Whispers."

Lira stood, her heart racing as the group pressed onward. The forest opened up before them, revealing the entrance to the valley. Tall, jagged cliffs rose on either side, casting long shadows over the path. Mist curled along the ground, and the whispers grew louder, filling the air with an eerie hum.

The Valley of Whispers was both breathtaking and foreboding. Wildflowers bloomed in every color imaginable, their delicate petals swaying in the breeze. Streams of silver light filtered through the mist, creating a dreamlike landscape. But despite the beauty, there was an undeniable tension in the air—a sense that something ancient and powerful watched them from the shadows.

"This place is incredible," Anya breathed, taking in the sight. "But... I feel like we're being watched."

"You're not imagining it," Lira replied, her hand instinctively moving toward the orb in her pocket. The essence within it pulsed faintly, reacting to the energy of the valley. "Something's here."

They continued down the winding path, the mist thickening around them. The whispers became clearer, almost as if they were trying to communicate, though the words remained indecipherable. Every now and then, the shadows seemed to shift, as if figures were moving just beyond their vision.

Suddenly, Kiran stopped, his eyes wide with fear. "Did you hear that?"

The group paused, scanning their surroundings. At first, there was only silence—then, a low growl echoed from the mist. Lira's heart leapt into her throat as a dark shape emerged from the fog, moving with an unnatural grace.

It was a creature unlike anything she had ever seen. Its body was shrouded in black mist, and its eyes glowed with an eerie light. The whispers seemed to intensify around it, as if it were the source of the valley's ghostly voices.

"We have to move," Orion said urgently, his voice tense. "Now!"

The group broke into a run, the creature close behind. Lira's pulse raced as they weaved through the misty landscape, the whispers growing louder with every step. It was as if the valley itself was trying to slow them down, pulling them deeper into its embrace.

They darted between towering rocks and thick underbrush, the creature never far behind. Lira's breath came in ragged gasps as she tried to focus on the path ahead, but the shadows seemed to shift and twist, making it difficult to find their way.

"This way!" Orion shouted, leading them toward a narrow path that cut between two cliffs.

Lira followed, her legs burning with exhaustion. As they reached the narrow passage, the creature let out a guttural roar, but it couldn't follow them through the tight space. They emerged on the other side, gasping for breath as the whispers began to fade.

For a moment, all was silent. Then, a faint light appeared ahead of them, glowing softly in the mist.

"The Heartstone," Lira whispered, her heart pounding with anticipation.

They moved cautiously toward the light, and as they approached, the mist parted to reveal a large stone pedestal. Atop it rested the Heartstone, glowing with a soft, ethereal light. It was a perfect sphere of pale crystal, pulsing gently as if alive with power.

Lira stepped forward, her hand trembling as she reached for it. The moment her fingers brushed the surface, a warmth spread through her, filling her with a sense of hope and strength unlike anything she had ever felt before.

"This is it," she said softly, her voice filled with awe. "This is what we need to defeat the Shade."

Orion and the others gathered around, their faces lit by the soft glow of the Heartstone. "It's beautiful," Anya whispered, her eyes wide with wonder.

But before they could celebrate, the ground beneath them rumbled. The whispers grew louder, more frantic, and the mist began to swirl violently around them.

"Something's coming," Orion warned, his voice tense. "We need to leave —now!"

The ground shook beneath their feet, and the mist seemed to come alive, swirling faster and faster. Lira clutched the Heartstone to her chest, its warmth seeping into her as if it were trying to calm her racing heart. But the danger was palpable—whatever was coming wasn't going to let them leave the Valley of Whispers so easily.

"Run!" Lira shouted, her voice barely audible over the deafening roar of the wind.

The group sprinted back toward the narrow path, but the mist thickened, obscuring their vision. It seemed to twist and curl around them, turning the landscape into a maze. The whispers were louder now, insistent and almost angry, as if the valley itself was protesting their intrusion.

Lira's heart pounded as she struggled to keep her bearings, her grip on the Heartstone tightening. She could hear Orion shouting orders, trying to guide the group through the confusion, but the mist was disorienting, and the growls from behind suggested the creature hadn't given up its pursuit.

Suddenly, a figure emerged from the mist—not the creature, but something far more familiar. It was her mother. Or at least, it looked like her mother, standing just a few feet away, smiling gently.

"Lira, you're safe now. Come back home," the figure said, her voice soft and reassuring.

Lira froze, confusion clouding her mind. This couldn't be real. Her mother was gone, lost to the sickness years ago. But the voice, the look in her eyes—it was so real, so comforting.

"Lira!" Orion's voice cut through the fog, snapping her back to reality. He grabbed her arm, pulling her away from the illusion. "Don't look at it! It's the valley—it's playing tricks on your mind!"

Lira blinked, and the figure of her mother dissolved into mist, vanishing as quickly as it had appeared. She gasped, the weight of the illusion sinking in. The Valley of Whispers wasn't just a place of beauty and danger—it was testing them, exploiting their deepest fears and desires.

"We have to keep moving," Orion urged, his grip on her arm firm. "The Heartstone is what it wants. We need to get out of here before it turns on us."

Lira nodded, shaking off the lingering sense of longing the illusion had left behind. She could still feel the warmth of the Heartstone, but now it seemed heavier, as if it carried the weight of responsibility. The valley wasn't just testing her—it was trying to break her resolve.

As they ran, the whispers around them grew more intense, pulling at their minds, conjuring images and voices of loved ones long gone or desires unfulfilled. Anya suddenly stumbled, clutching her head. "No... it's not real. It's not real!" she cried, backing away from something only she could see.

Lira rushed to her side, grabbing her shoulders. "Anya, look at me! None of it is real—it's the valley trying to trick you!"

Anya's eyes were wide, filled with fear, but she nodded as she regained her composure. Together, they continued forward, the oppressive mist making it harder to see and hear anything beyond their own frantic breaths.

Ahead of them, Kiran shouted. "This way!" His voice was barely audible through the howling winds. He waved frantically, motioning toward a faint opening in the mist that led back to the narrow path.

The group gathered their strength and ran toward him, the rumbling beneath their feet growing stronger with every step. Just as they reached the path, the ground cracked, splitting open with a thunderous roar. A deep chasm formed, separating them from their only exit.

Lira's heart sank. "What do we do now?" she cried, staring at the wide gap between them and the safety of the narrow passage.

Orion glanced around desperately. "We can't turn back. We'll have to jump."

The chasm was at least six feet across, and the mist swirled violently below, as if it were a living thing, waiting to swallow them whole. Lira's legs felt weak, but she knew they had no other choice.

"I'll go first," Orion said, stepping back to get a running start. With a powerful leap, he soared over the gap and landed on the other side, barely catching his balance.

"Come on, you can do it!" he shouted, holding out his hand.

Anya was next, her breath shaky as she gathered her courage. She jumped, and Orion caught her hand, pulling her to safety.

Lira's heart raced as she prepared for her own jump, clutching the Heartstone tightly. She took a deep breath, ran, and leapt across, her feet barely clearing the edge. Orion grabbed her arm, pulling her the rest of the way as she stumbled forward, gasping for air.

Kiran was the last to jump, but as he took his leap, the ground beneath him gave way. His hand shot out desperately, and Orion caught him at the last second, hauling him up before the mist could claim him.

They stood on the other side, breathing heavily, their hearts pounding in their chests. The whispers had quieted, but the mist still hung thick around them, an ever-present reminder of the valley's power.

"Is everyone okay?" Lira asked, glancing around at her friends. They all nodded, though their faces were pale and strained.

"We have to keep moving," Orion said, helping Kiran to his feet. "The valley won't stop until we're out."

The path ahead was narrow, but it seemed to lead toward a clearing where the mist wasn't as thick. The group moved cautiously, their nerves on edge, knowing the valley could strike again at any moment.

Finally, after what felt like hours of walking, they reached the edge of the valley. The mist began to thin, and the oppressive whispers faded into the distance. The sunlight broke through the clouds, and they found themselves standing on a high ridge overlooking a vast, green plain.

"We made it," Lira whispered, relief flooding through her as she gazed out at the peaceful landscape below.

Orion stood beside her, his hand resting on her shoulder. "We're not out of danger yet," he reminded her softly. "But we have the Heartstone now. That's what matters."

Lira nodded, holding the glowing crystal in her hands. It still radiated warmth, and she could feel its power pulsing through her. They had survived the Valley of Whispers, but the real battle was still ahead of them.

As the group began their descent down the ridge, Lira's thoughts turned to the Shade. It was only a matter of time before it returned, stronger and more dangerous than ever. But now, with the Heartstone, they had a chance—a chance to fight back, to protect their world from the darkness.

And in that moment, Lira realized something else. The journey had brought them closer, forging bonds that went beyond friendship. She glanced at Orion, who was walking just ahead of her, his presence steady and reassuring. A part of her had begun to rely on him in ways she hadn't anticipated.

The connection between them had deepened, shaped by the trials they had faced together. It wasn't love yet—not in the traditional sense—but it was something powerful, something undeniable. And as they prepared for the battles ahead, Lira couldn't help but wonder where that connection would lead.

But for now, their focus was clear. The Heartstone pulsed in her hands, a beacon of hope in the face of the coming storm. And with it, they would be ready to face whatever darkness awaited them.

11

The Gathering Storm

The descent from the Valley of Whispers had been uneventful, but an eerie stillness lingered in the air. As Lira, Orion, and the others made their way down the ridge, the oppressive feeling of the valley behind them slowly lifted, replaced by a heavy anticipation of what lay ahead.

The Heartstone continued to pulse in Lira's hands, its glow faint in the daylight but constant, as if it were alive. She could feel the connection growing stronger the closer they got to the plain below. It wasn't just a relic—it was a source of immense power, a conduit to something ancient, something that had been waiting to awaken for a long time.

"We need to rest soon," Anya said, her voice weary as she glanced at the horizon. "We've been moving since dawn."

Orion nodded, his sharp eyes scanning the landscape ahead. "There's a village at the edge of the plain. We can reach it by nightfall if we keep a steady pace."

Lira could sense the weariness in her friends, but she couldn't ignore the urgency clawing at her. The Shade was still out there, lurking, waiting for its moment to strike. She felt it more strongly now—a dark presence that seemed to move closer the stronger the Heartstone became. And with each pulse of the stone, her connection to it deepened.

As they walked, Kiran, usually the most talkative, was silent, his eyes fixed on the path ahead. Lira couldn't help but notice the way his gaze lingered on the Heartstone, a flicker of uncertainty in his expression.

"Kiran?" she asked quietly, walking beside him. "Is something bothering you?"

He shook his head at first, but then sighed, his voice low. "It's just... the Heartstone. There's something about it. Don't you feel it, too? Like it's pulling us toward something?"

Lira hesitated. She had felt the pull, but she hadn't spoken about it, unsure of what it meant. "I do," she admitted. "But I don't think it's something to fear. The Heartstone is powerful, yes, but it feels like it's on our side. Like it wants to help us."

Kiran nodded, though his face remained troubled. "I hope you're right. But there's something about it... something I can't shake."

Before Lira could respond, Orion called out from ahead. "We're close."

The group pushed forward, and soon, the village came into view. It was a small settlement nestled at the base of a rolling hill, its stone buildings bathed in the warm glow of the setting sun. Smoke rose lazily from chimneys, and the scent of burning wood drifted through the air, bringing with it a sense of comfort and safety.

As they approached, an elderly man greeted them at the village gates. His weathered face broke into a smile as he took in the sight of the weary travelers.

"Welcome, strangers. You look like you could use some rest," he said kindly. "The inn has warm beds and hot food. You're welcome to stay the night."

"Thank you," Orion replied, his voice grateful. "We've had a long journey."

The group entered the village and made their way to the inn. The warm fire crackling in the hearth and the smell of fresh bread made Lira's stomach rumble, a reminder of how long it had been since they'd had a proper meal. As they settled at a table, the tension in the group seemed to ease, the atmosphere more relaxed now that they were safe, if only for the night.

But as they ate and talked quietly among themselves, Lira couldn't shake the feeling that they were being watched. She glanced around the inn, her eyes scanning the faces of the other patrons. There was nothing overtly suspicious, but the hairs on the back of her neck stood on end.

"Do you feel that?" she whispered to Orion, who sat beside her.

He nodded, his gaze sharp. "We're not alone."

Just as he spoke, the door to the inn swung open, and a figure stepped inside. Cloaked in black, with a hood drawn low over their face, they moved silently across the room, taking a seat at the far corner. The room seemed to grow colder as the figure entered, and Lira's grip on the Heartstone tightened instinctively.

The others had noticed the stranger, too, their conversations halting as they exchanged uneasy glances. The figure remained motionless, seemingly uninterested in the group—but Lira knew better. This wasn't a coincidence. The Shade's influence was near.

"We should leave," Kiran muttered, his voice low.

"No," Orion said, his voice calm but firm. "We stay. If this is who I think it is, running will only draw attention."

Lira's heart pounded as the tension in the room thickened. She could feel the Heartstone pulsing in time with her racing pulse, its warmth a steady reminder of the power she held. But even with the Heartstone, she couldn't shake the feeling that they were in grave danger.

The stranger finally spoke, their voice a low, gravelly whisper. "You carry something powerful." Their words seemed to slice through the air, cutting through the silence.

Lira swallowed hard, her hand instinctively moving to the Heartstone. "Who are you?"

The figure lifted their head slightly, revealing pale, scarred skin beneath the hood. "I am one who seeks what you hold," they said, their eyes glowing faintly in the dim light. "But it does not belong to you."

Orion stood slowly, his hand resting on the hilt of his blade. "The Heartstone is not yours to claim."

The figure's lips curled into a cold smile. "Perhaps not yet. But it will be."

The air in the inn seemed to thicken, the shadows growing longer as the stranger's presence filled the room with an unnatural darkness. Lira's heart raced as she realized the truth—the figure wasn't human. It was a servant of the Shade.

"We're leaving," Orion said quietly, his voice tense. "Now."

The group stood as one, moving quickly toward the door. But the stranger didn't move to stop them. Instead, they simply watched, their eyes following Lira as she clutched the Heartstone tightly to her chest.

As they stepped outside into the cool night air, Lira could still feel the stranger's gaze on her, a cold, lingering presence that sent shivers down her spine. The Heartstone pulsed again, brighter this time, as if it, too, had sensed the danger.

"We're being hunted," Lira whispered, her voice barely audible.

Orion nodded grimly. "And the real battle has only just begun."

12

A New Ally

The group moved quickly through the village, keeping their heads low and their hands close to their weapons. Lira's pulse echoed the rhythm of her footsteps as the sense of being watched never left her. The stranger in the inn had not followed them, but their presence lingered like a cold shadow at their backs.

They made it to the outskirts of the village and regrouped near a small grove of trees. The night was quiet, save for the occasional rustle of leaves in the wind, but there was no time to rest.

"What was that thing?" Anya asked, her eyes wide with fear.

Orion shook his head. "A servant of the Shade. It's been tracking us."

"But why didn't it attack?" Kiran questioned, still glancing nervously over his shoulder.

Orion frowned. "It was gauging our strength. It knows we're dangerous now, especially with the Heartstone."

Lira stared down at the glowing crystal in her hands. She had felt the weight of its power grow with each passing day, but now she understood its true significance. The

Heartstone wasn't just a tool or a relic—it was a weapon. And the Shade wanted it back.

"We can't stay here," Orion said, his voice firm. "We need to move and find shelter away from the villages. The Shade's servants will keep coming."

But just as he finished speaking, a figure stepped out from the shadows of the trees, their hands raised in a gesture of peace.

"Wait!" the figure called softly, their voice urgent but nonthreatening. "I'm not here to hurt you."

Immediately, Orion drew his sword, stepping in front of Lira and the others. "Who are you?" he demanded.

The figure stepped closer, and as they emerged into the moonlight, Lira saw that it was a woman, her long dark hair tied back, her eyes sharp and focused. She wore travel-worn clothes, but there was something about her presence that commanded attention.

"My name is Nyla," she said, her voice calm but filled with purpose. "And I'm here to help you."

Lira, still gripping the Heartstone, stepped forward cautiously. "How do we know you're not one of the Shade's servants?"

Nyla's eyes softened slightly, as if she understood their fear. "Because I've been fighting against the Shade for years. And I know more about the Heartstone than you think."

Lira felt a surge of curiosity but also suspicion. "Why should we trust you?"

"Because if you don't, you'll be dead by morning," Nyla said bluntly. "The Shade's servants are coming for you, and you won't survive the night without my help."

Orion didn't lower his sword, but he studied Nyla carefully. "You seem to know a lot about us."

"I've been watching you since you entered the Valley of Whispers," she admitted, her gaze steady. "The Heartstone is awakening, and that's drawn a lot of attention—both good and bad."

Lira exchanged a glance with Orion. Nyla's words made sense, but there was still a nagging doubt in her mind. The Heartstone pulsed again, as if responding to the woman's presence.

"How do you know about the Heartstone?" Lira asked cautiously.

Nyla smiled, though there was little warmth in it. "Because I've been looking for it for a long time. It was lost when the first war with the Shade ended, and now that you've found it, the balance of power is shifting."

She stepped closer, lowering her hands as if to show she meant no harm. "I know how to use it. How to unlock its true potential. But if you want to stand a chance against the Shade, you're going to need my help."

Orion looked skeptical, but Lira couldn't ignore the sense of truth in Nyla's words. There was something about her—an intensity, a knowledge—that made Lira believe she might be their best chance.

"What do you want from us?" Lira asked, her voice steady despite the turmoil inside her.

Nyla's gaze locked with hers. "I want to destroy the Shade as much as you do. But we don't have much time. The more the Heartstone awakens, the more attention it draws. The servants you saw tonight were just scouts. The real danger is coming."

Kiran, who had been silent up until now, finally spoke up. "How do we know you're telling the truth?"

Nyla turned to him, her eyes hard. "You don't. But you've seen what the Shade can do. If you think you can fight it without the knowledge I have, then go ahead. But I promise you, you won't make it far."

Lira felt the weight of her decision pressing down on her. The Heartstone thrummed with energy in her hands, as if urging her to choose wisely. They had come so far, but they still didn't fully understand what they were up against. And time was running out.

Finally, Lira took a deep breath. "We'll hear you out," she said, her voice firm. "But if this is a trick, we won't hesitate to defend ourselves."

Nyla nodded, a flicker of respect crossing her face. "Fair enough."

Orion reluctantly lowered his sword but remained on guard. "Where do we go from here?"

Nyla glanced at the horizon, her eyes narrowing. "There's a place—a sanctuary hidden from the Shade's influence. It's where we'll be safe to prepare for what's coming. But it's a dangerous journey, and the Shade will try to stop us."

"Then we'd better get moving," Lira said, determination settling in her chest. The Heartstone pulsed again, and this time, it felt as though it was guiding her, pushing her forward.

With Nyla leading the way, the group set off into the night, leaving the village behind. The road ahead was uncertain, and the danger was greater than ever before, but Lira knew one thing for sure—they couldn't turn back now.

As they disappeared into the darkness, Lira cast one last glance over her shoulder, the memory of the stranger in the inn still fresh in her mind. The Shade was watching, waiting, and they were walking straight into its trap.

But this time, they wouldn't be alone.

13

Shadows and Secrets

The moon hung high in the sky as Lira, Orion, Kiran, Anya, and Nyla traveled deeper into the forest. The air was thick with the scent of pine and damp earth, and the sounds of the night filled their ears—an orchestra of rustling leaves and distant animal calls. Despite the beauty surrounding them, an unease lingered in the air.

"Are you sure this sanctuary is safe?" Anya asked, her voice laced with apprehension. "What if the Shade finds us?"

Nyla glanced back at her, her expression serious. "It's hidden from the Shade's servants. But we must move quickly. They'll sense our presence soon."

Lira could feel the Heartstone's energy humming softly in her grasp, almost like a heartbeat, guiding her through the darkness. She found comfort in its warmth, but also a growing sense of urgency. Each step felt like a countdown to something inevitable.

As they walked, Nyla began to share more about her own experiences fighting against the Shade. "I lost my family to the darkness," she said quietly, her gaze fixed on the path ahead. "They were taken by its servants while I was too weak to help. Since then, I've dedicated my life to fighting it, to finding the Heartstone."

Lira felt a pang of sympathy for Nyla. "I'm sorry. That must have been terrible."

Nyla nodded but didn't elaborate further. "The Shade feeds on fear and despair. It grows stronger when we are divided, when we lose hope. That's why we need to stay united. Trust each other."

As they continued, Kiran fell into step beside Lira, his expression pensive. "What do you think about her?" he asked quietly.

"I think she's been through a lot," Lira replied, glancing at Nyla ahead of them. "But I also think we need her knowledge. We can't fight the Shade alone."

Kiran nodded, but his brow furrowed. "I just hope we don't regret this decision."

Before Lira could respond, a low growl echoed through the trees, stopping them in their tracks. The group froze, hearts racing. Shadows moved among the branches, shifting and swirling like smoke.

"Stay close," Orion commanded, his voice steady as he drew his sword. "We may have company."

Nyla's eyes narrowed, scanning the darkened forest. "It's the Shade's servants. They've caught our scent."

Lira's heart raced as she tightened her grip on the Heartstone. "What do we do?"

"Form a circle," Orion instructed, positioning himself protectively in front of Lira and Anya. "We stand together."

The shadows thickened, and from the darkness emerged figures cloaked in black, their eyes glowing with malevolence. Lira could feel the dread rising in her chest as they advanced, surrounding the group.

"Draw your weapons!" Nyla shouted, her voice fierce. "We fight!"

With a rush of adrenaline, Lira pulled out her dagger, its blade gleaming in the moonlight. Kiran readied his own weapon, and Anya stood firm beside them, despite the fear etched on her face.

The first servant lunged at Orion, who countered with a swift strike. The creature staggered back but quickly regained its footing, snarling as it advanced again. Lira's breath quickened as more servants joined the fray, their movements fluid and eerily silent.

Nyla moved with practiced ease, her dagger slicing through the air. "Aim for the heart!" she shouted. "That's their weakness!"

Lira fought alongside her friends, every instinct screaming to survive. She could feel the Heartstone's energy rising within her, coursing through her veins. Each time she struck, a pulse of power surged from the Heartstone, fueling her resolve.

"Keep moving!" Orion shouted, deflecting another blow. "We need to break through their ranks!"

With each swing of her dagger, Lira felt more in tune with the Heartstone's magic. She began to understand how it connected her to the battle, empowering her with each heartbeat. "Kiran, to your left!" she called, dodging a dark figure that lunged toward her.

But the numbers were overwhelming. The servants seemed to emerge from every shadow, relentless in their assault. Lira glanced at her friends, their faces grim but determined. They were fighting for their lives, and failure was not an option.

Just as despair began to creep into her heart, the Heartstone pulsed fiercely, illuminating the darkness around them. Lira felt a rush of energy surge through her, and in that moment, she understood. The Heartstone was more than just a weapon; it was a source of light against the encroaching shadows.

"Together!" Lira shouted, raising the Heartstone high. "We can push them back!"

Orion, Kiran, and Anya joined her, forming a line of defense. The Heartstone glowed brighter, casting a warm light that pushed the shadows back, illuminating the twisted faces of the Shade's servants.

With renewed strength, Lira channeled the Heartstone's energy, focusing it into a beam of light that surged toward the nearest servant. The creature recoiled, shrieking as the light pierced through its form. The others faltered, hesitation creeping into their darkened hearts.

"Now!" Nyla urged, moving in tandem with Lira's newfound power. The group launched their attack, striking as one. Blades and light combined, cutting through the darkness with fierce determination.

One by one, the servants fell, their forms dissolving into wisps of shadow. The remaining creatures hesitated, sensing the shift in the battle's tide.

"Don't let up!" Orion yelled, driving forward with relentless fury. "We can't let them regroup!"

With each swing, Lira felt her connection to the Heartstone deepen, its energy flowing into her, filling her with light and courage. She pushed forward, determined to protect her friends and vanquish the darkness.

Finally, as the last of the Shade's servants fell, silence enveloped them. Breathing heavily, the group stood together, hearts racing in the aftermath of the battle.

"We did it," Anya said, her voice shaky but triumphant. "We actually did it."

Lira lowered her dagger, glancing at her friends, who wore expressions of disbelief and relief. The Heartstone pulsed gently in her hands, a reassuring presence in the chaos.

Nyla took a step forward, her gaze steady. "You're stronger than you realize. The Heartstone has chosen well."

"What do we do now?" Kiran asked, wiping sweat from his brow.

Nyla looked toward the path ahead, determination etched on her face. "Now we continue to the sanctuary. But we must be vigilant. This fight was only the beginning. The Shade will not give up so easily."

As they resumed their journey, Lira felt a new sense of purpose ignite within her. They had faced the darkness and survived. The Heartstone was more than just a relic—it was a beacon of hope, and she would wield it to protect her friends and defeat the Shade once and for all.

But in the depths of the forest, unseen eyes were watching, waiting for their next move. The real battle was far from over, and Lira knew they had to prepare for whatever horrors lay ahead.

14
The Sanctuary

As dawn approached, the forest began to brighten with hues of orange and gold. The group walked in silence, each lost in their thoughts, processing the fight they had just endured. Lira felt a renewed sense of determination, her grip firm on the Heartstone, which now pulsed softly at her side.

"Are we almost there?" Anya asked, glancing nervously at Nyla, who led the way with confidence.

Nyla nodded, her expression resolute. "Just a little further. The sanctuary is well hidden, protected by ancient magic. The Shade can't easily breach its defenses."

"Ancient magic?" Kiran repeated, curiosity piquing in his tone. "What does that mean?"

"It means the sanctuary was built by those who fought against the Shade long before us," Nyla explained. "It's a place where the light still remains, a bastion of hope amidst the darkness. It will give us the time we need to prepare and plan our next steps."

Lira felt a surge of hope at Nyla's words. A sanctuary meant safety, a place to rest and regroup. It was exactly what they needed after the harrowing battle.

As they pushed through the underbrush, a clearing emerged ahead, bathed in soft morning light. In the center stood a majestic tree, its branches sprawling wide and its leaves shimmering with iridescent colors. It looked like a painting come to life, a beacon of tranquility amidst the chaotic world outside.

"This is it," Nyla said, her voice filled with awe. "Welcome to the Sanctuary of Eldara."

Lira stepped into the clearing, her breath catching in her throat. The air felt charged with magic, a palpable energy that tingled against her skin. "It's beautiful," she whispered, taking in the sight of the ancient tree, which seemed to pulse with life itself.

Orion stepped forward, examining the area. "But how do we know we're truly safe here?"

Nyla smiled, walking closer to the tree. "The sanctuary has powerful wards. As long as we remain inside its boundaries, the Shade's servants cannot enter. But we must remain vigilant. The wards will not hold forever, especially now that they know we're here."

With a wave of her hand, Nyla gestured for them to gather around the tree. "Come, sit with me. We need to discuss our next move."

They formed a circle at the base of the tree, the Heartstone resting in the center, glowing faintly in the morning light. Lira could feel the energy radiating from it, connecting her to her friends and the sanctuary itself.

"First, we need to understand what we're dealing with," Nyla said, her voice steady. "The Shade is more than just a dark force; it has a mind of its own. It will seek to exploit our fears, our weaknesses. It will try to turn us against one another."

"Do you really think it can do that?" Kiran asked, skepticism in his tone. "We've been through so much together."

Nyla nodded, her expression serious. "Fear is a powerful weapon. It can cloud your judgment, make you question everything. We need to trust each other completely. It's the only way we'll succeed."

Lira felt a weight settle on her heart. "What if it gets to us? What if we can't hold on to that trust?"

"That's why we have to train," Nyla said, her gaze unwavering. "We need to learn how to harness the Heartstone's power. I can teach you how to focus your energies, how to channel the light within you. But it requires dedication and commitment."

"Count me in," Kiran said, his expression resolute. "I'm not letting the Shade win."

Anya nodded, determination flickering in her eyes. "Me too. We can't back down now."

Lira glanced at Orion, who seemed lost in thought. "What about you?" she asked. "Are you with us?"

He met her gaze, and for a moment, she felt an unspoken connection between them. "I'll do whatever it takes to protect you all," he said finally. "But I need to know how to wield this power too."

Nyla smiled, her eyes sparkling with approval. "Good. We have a lot of work ahead of us. Training will begin at dawn tomorrow, but for now, let's take some time to rest and gather our strength."

As the group settled into the sanctuary, Lira felt a mixture of relief and apprehension. They had found a safe haven, but the looming threat of the Shade still hung over them like a storm cloud.

That evening, as they prepared a small meal together, Lira felt a sense of camaraderie beginning to blossom among them. They shared stories and laughter, the tension from the previous night slowly dissipating. It was a moment of respite, a brief escape from the darkness they faced.

But as the sun dipped below the horizon, casting long shadows across the clearing, Lira couldn't shake the feeling that they were being watched. She glanced around, but the sanctuary felt peaceful, the magic wrapping around them like a protective cloak.

15

Whispers in the Night

As twilight descended over the sanctuary, Lira found herself wandering away from the group, drawn by the soft glow of the Heartstone. The air was cool, and the first stars twinkled in the evening sky, casting a gentle light over the clearing. She needed a moment to gather her thoughts, to breathe and reflect on the journey ahead.

Orion noticed her absence and followed quietly, his footsteps soft against the forest floor. When he found her near the Heartstone, its light shimmering against her face, he couldn't help but admire her. The glow illuminated her features, and for a moment, he was captivated by the way she seemed to embody both strength and vulnerability.

"Hey," he said, his voice low and warm. "You alright?"

Lira turned, surprised but pleased to see him. "Yeah, just needed a moment alone to think." She gestured toward the Heartstone. "It's beautiful, isn't it?"

"More than beautiful," Orion replied, stepping closer. "It's powerful. And so are you." His gaze held hers, and Lira felt her heart flutter at the intensity in his eyes.

"I'm just trying to keep it together," Lira admitted, her voice barely above a whisper. "Sometimes it feels like the weight of the world is on my shoulders."

"You're not alone in this," Orion said, taking another step closer. "We're all in this together. But you... you carry a strength I've never seen before." He paused, his expression serious. "I believe in you, Lira."

His words wrapped around her like a warm embrace, and Lira felt a rush of emotions. "I wish I had your confidence," she confessed, her gaze dropping to the ground. "You make it look so easy."

"It's not easy," he admitted, his voice softening. "But having you by my side makes everything feel possible. You give me strength, too."

Lira met his eyes, her heart racing. "Really? I never thought..."

"Of course," he interrupted gently. "It's the truth. You light up the darkest places, Lira. I've seen it happen, even today during the battle. The way you faced the shadows... it was inspiring."

In that moment, the air between them thickened with unspoken feelings. Lira's heart pounded as she stepped closer to him. "Orion, I..."

Before she could finish her thought, he reached out, brushing a loose strand of hair behind her ear. The simple touch sent shivers down her spine, igniting a spark of warmth in her chest. "What were you going to say?" he asked, his voice barely above a whisper.

"I was going to say that you make me feel... safe. Even in the darkest moments." Lira felt a blush creeping up her cheeks. "And I don't want to lose that."

His gaze softened, and in that moment, the world around them faded away. "You won't lose me," he promised, stepping closer until there was barely any space left between them. "I'm not going anywhere, Lira. Not now, not ever."

The intensity of his gaze sent her heart racing, and she felt a magnetic pull toward him. "Orion..."

Sure! Here's the continuation of Chapter 15, deepening the romantic moment between Lira and Orion:

"Orion..." Lira breathed, her voice trembling as she gazed up at him. The air was electric, filled with the unspoken tension that had been building between them for so long.

In that vulnerable moment, Lira could see all the battles they had faced reflected in his eyes—the fear, the determination, and the unwavering support. She felt a surge of courage and took another step closer, her heart racing. "I care about you. More than I ever thought I could."

He smiled softly, his expression filled with warmth. "I care about you too, Lira. You've become my anchor in all this chaos."

They stood there for a heartbeat longer, the world around them forgotten. Lira's heart raced as she realized how much she wanted to close the distance between them. The pull was undeniable, a force stronger than the looming shadows threatening their lives.

Then, with a sudden surge of bravery, Lira reached out and took his hand, intertwining her fingers with his. "I don't want to face the darkness alone," she admitted, her voice steady now. "I want to face it with you."

Orion's grip tightened around her hand, and he stepped even closer, their bodies almost touching. "Then we will face it together, side by side. I promise."

As he spoke, Lira felt her breath hitch in her throat. The sincerity in his words resonated deep within her, and before she could think better of it, she found herself leaning in, drawn by an irresistible force.

Orion's eyes widened slightly, but he didn't pull away. Instead, he tilted his head slightly, encouraging her. And in that suspended moment, Lira closed the distance, their lips meeting in a soft, tentative kiss.

Time seemed to stand still. The world melted away, leaving just the two of them enveloped in warmth and light. The kiss was tentative at first, as if they were both testing the waters, but it quickly deepened, filled with the passion and urgency they had both been holding back. Lira felt a rush of emotions, a mix of relief, joy, and an exhilarating sense of connection.

When they finally pulled apart, breathless and wide-eyed, Lira couldn't help but smile. "Wow," she said, still caught in the moment.

Orion chuckled softly, his eyes sparkling with a mixture of surprise and delight. "Wow indeed."

Suddenly, the serenity of the sanctuary was interrupted by a distant rumble—a reminder of the looming threat of the Shade. Lira's heart sank as reality flooded back in. "We need to prepare," she said reluctantly, her heart still racing from their kiss.

Orion nodded, his expression shifting back to focus. "You're right. But we can't lose sight of what we have, Lira. You give me hope. Let's keep that close, even as we fight."

Lira squeezed his hand, grounding herself in the connection they had forged. "Together," she promised, her voice steady.

"Together," he echoed, a newfound determination in his gaze.

As they turned back toward the sanctuary, the Heartstone's light seemed to shine brighter, reflecting the strength of their bond. They would face whatever came next side by side, armed not just with magic but with the power of their shared feelings.

With their hearts intertwined, Lira and Orion stepped back into the fray, ready to confront the darkness ahead, knowing they had each other to rely on.

16
The Power Within

———◦♡◦———

The morning sun poured into the sanctuary, illuminating the ancient tree and casting dancing shadows on the forest floor. Lira felt invigorated as she joined her friends around the Heartstone, its glow still pulsing softly in the center of their circle. Today marked the beginning of their training, and Lira was ready to embrace the challenge.

Nyla stood at the forefront, her presence commanding as she prepared to lead them. "Today, we will learn to harness the Heartstone's energy and channel it into our abilities. Each of you has a unique gift; we need to identify and strengthen them."

"What if we can't do it?" Kiran asked, his brow furrowed with doubt. "What if we're not strong enough?"

"Strength comes from within," Nyla replied, her voice firm. "You must believe in yourselves and in each other. Fear will only weaken your resolve. Trust that the Heartstone will guide you."

Lira felt a swell of determination rise within her. They had faced the darkness and emerged victorious; there was no room for doubt now. She glanced at her friends, all of them ready to fight for their future.

"Let's begin," Nyla said, her eyes sparkling with excitement. "Close your eyes and take a deep breath. Focus on the Heartstone and let its energy flow through you."

Lira followed Nyla's instructions, closing her eyes and centering her thoughts. She focused on the warmth radiating from the Heartstone, allowing it to fill her with light and strength. In her mind, she envisioned her hopes and dreams—her desire to protect her home, her friends, and the world from the Shade.

As she immersed herself in the energy, Lira felt a connection form between herself and the Heartstone. Images began to dance in her mind: flashes of light, swirling colors, and the laughter of her friends. She could feel the power of the Heartstone pulsing in rhythm with her heartbeat, a reassuring presence guiding her.

When she opened her eyes, the world around her seemed to shimmer with new possibilities. "I feel it," Lira whispered, glancing at Nyla. "I can feel the energy."

"Good," Nyla said, a smile spreading across her face. "Now, let's put that energy to use. Focus on a single thought or emotion, and channel it into a beam of light. Picture it extending from your hands, just like the Heartstone."

Kiran was next to her, concentrating hard. "Here goes nothing," he muttered, his brow furrowed in determination. With a deep breath, he extended his hands outward. Lira watched in awe as a beam of shimmering light burst forth, illuminating the clearing.

"Nice one!" Anya cheered, her eyes wide with excitement. "I want to try!"

Nyla guided each of them through the process, helping them channel their unique energies into powerful beams of light. One by one, they stepped forward, and Lira felt the air thrum with magic as they practiced.

When it was Orion's turn, Lira felt her heart race. He stood tall and confident, eyes narrowed in focus. As he stretched his hands outward, a brilliant arc of light shot forth, swirling like a galaxy in motion. Lira gasped, captivated by the beauty of his magic.

"Wow, Orion!" she exclaimed. "That was incredible!"

"Thanks," he replied, a hint of a smile on his lips. But then he glanced at Nyla, a serious expression returning. "What if we can't control it? What if it backfires?"

Nyla stepped closer, placing a reassuring hand on his shoulder. "Control comes with practice. You all have the power within you; it's a matter of finding it and learning to harness it. Trust yourselves, and trust each other."

As they continued practicing, Lira found herself growing more confident. With each burst of light, she felt her connection to the Heartstone strengthen. It was as if she were a part of something greater, a force of magic intertwined with her friends.

But as they practiced, Lira couldn't shake the feeling that time was running out. The Shade would not be idle; they would come again, stronger and more determined.

17
Shadows Gather

That evening, as the sun dipped below the horizon, painting the sky in hues of orange and purple, Lira gathered with her friends around the Heartstone once more. They shared their progress and successes, but the air was thick with an unspoken tension.

"We're getting stronger," Kiran said, glancing at the glowing Heartstone. "But I still feel like we're not ready. The Shade will come for us again."

Nyla nodded, her expression serious. "You're right. We need to prepare for the worst. The Heartstone may provide us with power, but we also need strategies. The Shade is cunning; it will exploit our weaknesses if we let it."

"What do you suggest?" Anya asked, her brow furrowed with concern.

"Tonight, we'll set up a watch," Nyla replied. "We'll take turns keeping guard. I want you all to remain vigilant; if the Shade is near, we'll need to be ready to respond."

Lira felt a knot of anxiety tighten in her stomach. "What if we can't hold them off? What if they overwhelm us?"

"We won't let that happen," Orion said, his voice steady. "We're stronger together, and we'll fight for each other.

We've already faced the darkness and won."

Lira appreciated his confidence, but as night fell and the first stars appeared in the sky, she couldn't shake the feeling that something ominous was brewing just beyond the sanctuary's protective wards.

As the group settled into their watch rotation, Lira took the first shift. She sat on a log near the Heartstone, scanning the dark woods surrounding the sanctuary. The chirping of crickets filled the air, a soothing melody that belied the tension she felt within.

Her thoughts drifted to Orion. There was something about their connection that felt deeper than friendship. They had faced danger together, fought side by side, and with each passing moment, her feelings for him grew stronger. But in this uncertain world, could she afford to let those feelings flourish?

Suddenly, a rustling in the bushes snapped her back to reality. Lira strained to listen, her heart racing. Shadows danced at the edges of the clearing, and she squinted into the darkness, trying to make out any movement.

"Is someone there?" she called out, her voice steady despite the rising panic in her chest.

Silence followed, heavy and suffocating. Just as she began to doubt herself, a shape emerged from the trees. It was Nyla, her expression serious and urgent.

"Lira," she whispered, her voice low. "I felt a disturbance. The wards are weakening. We need to alert the others."

Lira's heart sank. "What does that mean?"

"It means the Shade may be closer than we thought. They've sensed the Heartstone's power, and they won't stop until they claim it."

Lira nodded, determination surging through her. "Let's wake the others. We can't let them take it from us."

They rushed back to the others, rousing Kiran and Anya from their sleep. Orion was already alert, his eyes sharp and focused. "What's happening?" he asked, his voice low and tense.

"Nyla felt a disturbance," Lira explained, her heart racing. "The wards are weakening. The Shade could be on their way."

"Then we must prepare," Orion said, stepping forward. "We need to defend the Heartstone. It's our only hope."

As they gathered their weapons and took positions around the Heartstone, Lira felt a surge of fear and determination. They had come too far to let the darkness win now. They would stand and fight, not just for the Heartstone, but for each other.

And as the first shadows of the Shade began to seep into the sanctuary, Lira took a deep breath, ready to face the darkness that threatened their newfound hope. She felt the energy of the Heartstone at her side, pulsing in sync with her heart. Together, they would be strong enough to fight back.

18
The Dark Assault

The air grew heavy with tension as the first whispers of the Shade seeped into the sanctuary. Shadows coalesced at the edges of the clearing, dark figures swirling like smoke, their forms shifting and undulating, seeking to infiltrate the light of the Heartstone.

"Stand your ground!" Nyla commanded, her voice ringing clear. She stepped forward, fierce determination radiating from her as she prepared to channel the energy of the Heartstone.

Lira felt her heart pounding in her chest, her palms clammy around her weapon. She exchanged a quick glance with Orion, who stood nearby, eyes narrowed and fierce. There was an unspoken understanding between them: they would face this darkness together.

As the first wave of shadowy figures lunged forward, Nyla unleashed a brilliant beam of light from her hands. It sliced through the darkness, illuminating the clearing and sending the shadowy figures reeling back with anguished hisses.

"Now, everyone! Focus your energies!" Nyla shouted. "Channel the Heartstone's light!"

Lira closed her eyes, envisioning the warmth of the Heartstone flowing through her, empowering her with its brilliance. She raised her hands, and a shimmering beam shot forth, joining Nyla's light and pushing back the encroaching shadows. Kiran and Anya followed suit, their energies combining to create a radiant barrier around the Heartstone.

The shadows writhed and screeched, but their fear only fueled Lira's determination. She could feel the magic within her, resonating with the Heartstone, urging her to dig deeper.

Orion stepped closer to her, his expression fierce and protective. "We need to keep the pressure on! Don't let them regroup!"

Lira nodded, her resolve hardening. "Together!"

With that, they unleashed a barrage of light, pushing the shadows further back, their cries mingling with the night air. But the Shade was relentless; for every shadow they pushed away, two more seemed to take its place.

"Lira, watch out!" Kiran shouted, pointing as a particularly large shadow lunged toward her, its claws outstretched.

Before she could react, Orion stepped in front of her, his own light flaring as he deflected the attack. The shadow hissed and recoiled, but it was clear they were outnumbered.

"We can't keep this up forever!" Anya exclaimed, panting as she struggled to maintain her focus. "There are too many!"

Nyla took a deep breath, her brow furrowing in concentration. "We need to amplify our magic! We can use the Heartstone as a conduit, but we have to trust each other completely."

"Trust?" Kiran asked, glancing at the shadows swirling around them. "Can we really do that?"

"Yes," Lira said, her voice steady. "We've already faced so much together. If we connect our powers, we can create a barrier strong enough to protect the Heartstone."

Nyla nodded, her eyes brightening with hope. "Exactly! We need to form a circle around the Heartstone, and as one, we'll channel our energies into it."

The group quickly formed a circle, their backs pressed against each other. Lira felt the warmth of Orion's energy beside her, a steadying presence in the chaos. Their fingers brushed, igniting a spark that made her heart flutter. She closed her eyes again, allowing herself to feel the connection between them.

"On three," Nyla instructed. "One... two... three!"

In unison, they raised their hands toward the Heartstone, channeling their magic through it. A radiant light burst forth, enveloping the sanctuary in a blinding glow. The shadows hesitated, swirling uneasily as the barrier expanded around them.

The light grew brighter and brighter until it burst like a supernova, scattering the shadows and forcing them back. Lira could feel the energy of her friends blending with her own, creating an unbreakable bond of trust and determination. But in that moment, all she could focus on was Orion, who stood beside her, their hands almost touching.

"Stay close to me!" Orion shouted over the din, his eyes fierce with determination. "We can't let them separate us!"

"I won't leave your side!" Lira called back, her heart swelling with warmth.

But the battle was relentless. The shadows writhed and screeched, and Lira felt the pull of darkness trying to seep into her mind, sowing seeds of doubt. She glanced at Orion, who was pushing against the shadows with all his might, and the sight of him fighting fiercely for their cause fueled her resolve.

"Orion!" she shouted, finding strength in his presence. "We can do this together!"

"Together!" he echoed, his voice a beacon of hope amidst the chaos.

As they unleashed another wave of light, Lira felt a deep connection with Orion, a bond forged through shared struggles and newfound love. The energy between them pulsed like a heartbeat, guiding their magic as it intertwined, creating a luminous shield that surged forward.

In the midst of the turmoil, Lira and Orion locked eyes, and for a brief moment, time stood still. The shadows faded into the background, and all that mattered was the connection they shared. They were fighting not just for their lives but for the love that had blossomed between them—a love that had the power to illuminate even the darkest corners of their world.

But the moment was Sure! Here's the continuation of Chapter 18, keeping the romantic focus while maintaining the tension of the battle:

But the moment was fleeting. The shadows surged forward again, their dark forms relentless, seeking to overwhelm the light. Lira felt a chill run through her as the darkness pressed closer, and she instinctively reached for Orion's hand, intertwining their fingers tightly.

"We can't let them break our focus!" she shouted, her heart racing. "We need to be stronger together!"

Orion nodded, his grip firm and reassuring. "Let's channel everything we have. No doubts, no fears—just our light!"

They closed their eyes, drawing strength from one another, feeling the warmth of their connection pulse between them. In that moment, the bond they shared became a source of power. Lira envisioned their energies merging, a brilliant golden light radiating from their intertwined hands, illuminating the dark space around them.

"On three, we unleash everything we've got," Nyla said, her voice steady amidst the chaos. "One... two... three!"

With a united cry, Lira and Orion released their magic, a brilliant wave of light erupting from their joined hands. The air crackled with energy as their combined powers surged forth, pushing the shadows back with blinding brilliance. Lira felt exhilarated, the rush of magic coursing through her veins, amplified by the presence of Orion beside her.

But just as they began to gain ground, a massive shadow figure lunged at them, its dark claws reaching for Lira. Time seemed to slow as she realized the threat; she had no choice but to react.

"Orion, look out!" Lira screamed, her heart pounding in her chest.

Without thinking, she stepped in front of him, raising her free hand to shield them both. As the shadow lunged, she could feel Orion's energy flaring behind her, protective and strong.

In that moment of sheer instinct, Lira's heart swelled with an overwhelming desire to protect the one person who had become her anchor in the storm. "I won't let them take you!" she shouted, determination fueling her resolve.

The dark figure collided with the light barrier they had created, the force sending ripples through the air. Lira could feel the pressure of its weight bearing down on her, but she held her ground, channeling every ounce of her energy into the barrier.

"Lira!" Orion's voice broke through, full of concern and urgency. "We have to push it back together!"

Feeling the connection between them, Lira nodded, drawing strength from their bond. "On three again! One... two... three!"

Together, they thrust their hands forward, and a wave of golden light exploded from their joined energies, pushing the shadow figure back. The creature screeched, its form disintegrating under the onslaught of their combined magic, scattering like ashes in the wind.

Breathless, Lira turned to Orion, who looked at her with a mixture of admiration and awe. "You were incredible!" he exclaimed, his voice filled with emotion. "You saved us."

"Only because you were there with me," Lira replied, her cheeks flushed, their eyes locked in an unbreakable gaze.

But before they could savor the moment, more shadows surged toward them, desperate to fill the void left by their fallen companion. The battle was far from over.

"Focus!" Nyla shouted, rallying the group. "We can't let our guard down!"

As the shadows pressed in, Lira felt a surge of adrenaline coursing through her. With Orion at her side, she could face anything. They stood shoulder to shoulder, hearts beating in sync as they prepared for the next wave of darkness.

With every pulse of magic they unleashed, Lira felt the love she had for Orion grow stronger, intertwining with their fight against the Shade. She knew they could overcome anything together, their bond a beacon of light amidst the encroaching darkness.

"Let's do this," Lira said, her voice steady.

"Together," Orion affirmed, a fierce determination glinting in his eyes.

They charged forward, their magic radiating around them, ready to face the shadows and whatever else the night would bring.

19

The Heartstone's Awakening

Chapter 19: The Heartstone's Awakening

But the battle was far from over. The shadows regrouped, swirling angrily, their howls mingling with the rustling leaves as if the very forest were in pain. Lira could sense their rage; they were no longer just mindless minions of the Shade but a united force, desperate to extinguish the light they feared.

"Keep your focus!" Nyla shouted, her voice a beacon of strength amid the chaos. "Don't let them break your concentration!"

Lira felt her heart racing, and she took a deep breath, channeling her fear into strength. The Heartstone pulsed beside her, its glow resonating with the rhythm of her heartbeat. She could feel the connection between them all, a thread of magic binding them as they stood together against the darkness.

With renewed determination, she raised her hands, willing the Heartstone's energy to flow through her. "We can't let them win! We have to push back harder!"

Orion stepped closer, his shoulder brushing against hers, sending a spark of warmth through her. "Together!" he declared, his voice low and steady, sending a shiver of anticipation down her spine.

As they moved together, the sanctuary glowed brighter, illuminating the edges of the forest. The shadows struggled against the onslaught, but their forms began to dissipate under the relentless light.

Just as victory seemed within reach, a massive shadow coalesced at the back of the dark horde, growing larger and darker than the others. It loomed ominously, and Lira felt a chill run down her spine. This was no mere shadow; it was the embodiment of the Shade's wrath, a creature of pure darkness that radiated malice.

"This one is different," Lira breathed, her voice barely above a whisper. "It's... stronger."

Orion turned to her, his expression fierce but laced with concern. "Stay close to me," he said, reaching for her hand and giving it a reassuring squeeze. "We'll face it together."

Nyla's expression hardened. "We need to focus our efforts. That shadow is the Shade's heart, the core of its darkness. If we can weaken it, we may break its hold over the others!"

"Then let's end this!" Orion shouted, his eyes blazing with intensity. "Together!"

With a fierce resolve, they formed a tighter circle around the Heartstone, channeling their magic into one concentrated point. Lira could feel the fear and determination of her friends blending into a singular force, but her thoughts kept drifting back to Orion. She could see the strength in him, but she also saw the vulnerability that he tried to hide.

"Now!" Nyla commanded.

"On three!" Lira echoed, adrenaline pumping through her veins. "One... two... three!"

They thrust their hands forward, a torrent of light erupting from the Heartstone. It pierced the gloom, striking the dark creature. It roared in fury, its form twisting as the light met its surface. But instead of retreating, it charged forward, seeking to engulf them in darkness.

"Focus!" Nyla shouted, her voice a steady anchor. "We can't let it consume us!"

As the darkness surged, Lira's heart raced. "We have to believe in the light!" she cried, channeling all her hope and determination into the Heartstone. "For each other! For our world!"

The light surged, blindingly brilliant, engulfing the shadow as they poured their energy into one final push. Lira felt the connection between them all—an unbreakable bond forged through trust and love.

In that moment, the Heartstone flared to life, a supernova of light that engulfed the clearing. The shadows screeched in terror as the darkness around them began to unravel. The massive shadow shrieked, flailing against the onslaught of brilliance.

Then, with a sound like shattering glass, the dark figure shattered into a million fragments, scattering into the night air. The remaining shadows flickered and dissolved, retreating into the depths of the forest as if the very fabric of the Shade's magic had been torn asunder.

20

Aftermath and Hope

As the light faded, Lira collapsed to her knees, breathless and trembling. The sanctuary, once filled with darkness, now radiated with a serene glow. The Heartstone pulsed gently, its warmth soothing her exhausted body.

Orion knelt beside her, concern etched across his features. "Are you alright?" His voice was soft, and his intense gaze sent warmth flooding through her.

"I... I think so," Lira panted, a smile breaking through her exhaustion. "We did it. We pushed them back!"

Nyla knelt beside them, her eyes sparkling with pride. "You all showed incredible strength. That was a remarkable display of unity. We're not just fighting for ourselves anymore; we're fighting for everyone who has suffered under the Shade's tyranny."

Kiran and Anya approached, their faces illuminated with triumph. "I can't believe we actually did it," Anya exclaimed, her voice a mixture of disbelief and joy. "We stood against the darkness and won!"

But as they celebrated, Lira felt a shadow of uncertainty settle over her. "But what about the Shade? It's not gone. It will come back."

Nyla nodded, her expression turning serious. "Yes, it will. The Shade is relentless, and we must prepare for its return. But now we have hope. We've proven that together, we can overcome even the darkest of forces."

Lira looked at her friends, the bonds between them stronger than ever. "We'll train harder," she vowed. "We'll learn to harness the Heartstone's power and protect our world."

Orion squeezed her hand, his eyes reflecting a determination that ignited a spark in her heart. "We'll face whatever comes next, together." He leaned in slightly, his breath warm against her cheek. "I promise to be right by your side, Lira."

Heat rushed to her cheeks at his words, and she looked up to meet his gaze. In that moment, the world around them faded, and it felt as if they were the only two left in existence. Lira's heart raced, the connection between them deepening in the aftermath of battle.

As the sun began to rise over the sanctuary, painting the sky with hues of pink and gold, Lira felt a renewed sense of purpose. The battle was just beginning, but with Orion beside her, she knew they could face any challenge the Shade threw at them.

And in that moment of hope and unity, Lira realized that love and friendship were the true light that would guide them through the darkness. Together, they would stand against the Shade, ready to protect their world and each other, no matter what the future held.

As they sat together, hands intertwined, Lira glanced at the Heartstone, glowing softly in the morning light. It was a symbol of their bond, a testament to the power of love and unity in the face of darkness.

"Together, we are stronger," she whispered, squeezing Orion's hand.

He smiled at her, a look of fierce determination mixed with warmth in his eyes. "Always."

And with that promise echoing in their hearts, they stood together, ready to face whatever awaited them beyond the sanctuary, their connection stronger than any shadow that threatened to engulf them.

Epilogue: A New Dawn

Months had passed since the climactic battle at the Sanctuary of Eldara. The dark forces of the Shade had been vanquished, leaving behind whispers of hope in a world that was slowly healing. Lira stood at the edge of a serene lake, the water mirroring the vibrant hues of dawn, each ripple reflecting the promise of a new beginning.

Orion approached, his presence warm and comforting as he slipped his arm around her shoulders, drawing her close. "You always seem to find the best views," he teased lightly, his voice wrapping around her like a soft embrace.

Lira smiled, turning to face him, her heart swelling at the sight of him. "I guess I'm just drawn to beauty. It reminds me of everything we fought for." Her gaze returned to the water, where the sun was just beginning to rise, casting golden rays that danced across the surface.

As they stood together, the world around them felt alive, yet all Lira could focus on was Orion. The warmth of his arm around her ignited a feeling deep within her, a sensation that had only grown stronger since their journey began. "You know," she said softly, "every time I see a sunrise like this, I remember how far we've come. And how much you mean to me."

Orion turned to her, his expression shifting from playful to earnest. "I never thought I could find something so precious in the midst of chaos. But you've become my light, Lira. In the darkest moments, it was your strength that kept me going."

Her heart raced as she met his gaze, the intensity of his words washing over her. "And you have shown me what it means to truly fight for something, to protect those we love.

I can't imagine facing anything without you by my side."

As the first rays of sunlight kissed their faces, Orion brushed a stray lock of hair behind her ear, his fingers lingering for a heartbeat longer than necessary. "Promise me, no matter what challenges we face in the future, we'll confront them together. I want to be with you, through every sunrise and every storm."

"I promise," she whispered, her voice barely audible against the soft rustling of leaves. In that moment, Lira felt an overwhelming sense of connection, a bond forged in the heat of battle that had blossomed into something profound.

The silence between them was thick with unspoken words, emotions that hung in the air like the dawn mist. Lira took a step closer, her heart pounding as she searched his eyes for reassurance. "Orion... I don't want to just fight alongside you. I want to build a life with you, beyond all of this."

His gaze softened, and a smile broke across his face, illuminating his features. "I want that too, more than anything. You've shown me the beauty in fighting for a future. With you, I see possibilities I never imagined."

As the sun broke free from the horizon, casting warm light around them, Lira felt the weight of their shared experiences lift. They had faced the darkness and emerged stronger, not just as warriors but as partners. The love that had grown between them was a shield against the remnants of fear that lingered from their battles.

"Let's go find our friends," Lira suggested, excitement bubbling within her. "We need to celebrate our victory together, but I also want to share our future with them."

"Lead the way," Orion replied, a grin spreading across his face, his eyes sparkling with hope.

Hand in hand, they walked back toward the village, their fingers intertwined, hearts beating in sync. With every step, Lira felt a sense of peace enveloping her. This was just the beginning, and she was ready to embrace the future with Orion by her side.

As they stepped into the warm embrace of the morning sun, Lira knew that their journey together had only just begun. With love as their guiding light, they would face whatever challenges lay ahead—together, forever united.